HYPED

← A Luke Novel →

Black Pearl Books Publishing

www.BLACKPEARLBOOKS.COM

A Luke Novel

Published By:

BLACK PEARL BOOKS INC.

3653-F FLAKES MILL ROAD – PMB 306
ATLANTA, GA 30034
404-735-3553

Copyright 2005 © Luke

All Black Pearl Books titles, imprints and distributed lines are available at special quantity discounts for bulk purchases for sales promotion, premiums, fund raising, educational or institutional use.

Special book excerpts or customized printings can also be created to fit specific needs. For details, write to Black Pearl Books: Attention Senior Publisher, 3653-F Flakes Mill Road, PMB-306, Atlanta, Georgia 30034 or visit website: www.BlackPearlBooks.com

FOR DISTRIBUTOR INFO & BULK ORDERING

Contact: **Black Pearl Books, Inc.**
3653-F Flakes Mill Road
PMB 306
Atlanta, Georgia 30034
404-735-3553

Discount Book-Club Orders via website:

www.BlackPearlBooks.com

ISBN: 0-9728005-6-5   LCCN: 2004195073

Publication Date: January 2005

Cover Credits

Design: CANDACEK. (WWW.CCWEBDEV.COM)

Acknowledgements

I'd like to start by giving thanks to God for his many blessing of creativity and vision. A special thanks goes out to my family for their unwavering love and support. My parents, Luke and Rhonda Thomas; my beautiful daughters Ariana and Jasmine; my brothers JohnPaul, Brandton and family; and my sister, Shoy and family. You guys are my true inspiration.

To my road dawg, Terry Mitchell; thanks for having my back from day one. And to my home girl Ersie Alexandre, your voice of motivation and encouragement has kept a brotha pressing forward to pursue the dream.

Much luv goes out to my magnificent editor Kimberly Hines, your edits were invaluable. Let's keep the best sellers rolling! A special thanks to Felicia Hurst and the rest of the family at BlackPearl Books. We're just getting started! To my homeboy Dexter "The Blade" Jackson, thanks for the tips in the gym. Keep shooting for that Mr. Olympia title!

Thanks to all of the authors that offered their support and guidance. Zane, you have an aficionado for life. Thanks for the good reviews and words of encouragement. Also a big thank you to all of the African American Bookstores for their support. A special shout to Reba Johnson of "Expressions" Bookstore in Jacksonville.

Last but most certainly not least, I'd like to thank all of my loyal readers, fans, and everyone who purchased this book. Your support is much appreciated, and I'm confident you'll enjoy this work. There will be more to come!

Peace Luke

HYPED

← A Luke Novel →

Black Pearl Books Publishing

www.BlackPearlBooks.com

Chapter One
Soul Man

"Yes! Yes! Yes!"

Maurice applied long strokes, and her screams came between short breaths.

"You...like...that?" Maurice punctuated every word with a deep thrust.

"Yes...I...like...it!" Her hips moved in tune with the Eric Benét groove emanating from the speakers positioned in the corners of the room.

Maurice maneuvered both of her legs onto his strong shoulders and increased his pace. "You...like...that?" he repeated, with more emphasis.

This time she could only answer with sensual sounds and moans. Maurice felt her body start to shake, and he knew that a full-fledged climax wasn't far behind. But he wasn't done with her yet.

"I...said...do...you...like--"

The annoying screech of the alarm clock brought Maurice LaSalle's entertaining dream to a sudden halt. He awoke from his stupor and wiped away the early-morning drool.

Squinting from the bright streaks of sunlight that peered through the blinds and rudely intruded upon his fantasy, Maurice's vision slowly began to come into focus. Being a child of the night, he really hated getting up early in the morning, especially on the weekends. He lay heavily on the snooze button.

Glancing over at the annoying red glow, which flashed nine o'clock, he could feel the effects of Hennessey tearing at his head.

"Damn, I really don't feel like doing this," he mumbled.

It was Saturday, and he would spend his morning volunteering at Twilight Arms, a senior citizen's community near the beach. His presence was welcomed by the lonely souls who called Twilight home. Most relatives left them there and forgot they existed, not bothering to pay them a visit.

The older guys were always elated when Maurice would stop by and spend a little time with them. They figured they could teach him a thing or two about life and help him take the narrow path instead of the wide road that led to nowhere. Each one had a story to tell and a lot of advice to give, so Maurice always kept an open mind and gratefully accepted the knowledge the old-school cats were willing to impart to him.

Maurice yawned loudly as he struggled to pull his 215-pound athletic physique out of bed. Standing 6 feet with razor-cut muscles protruding from his frame, he usually left a trail of drooling females in his wake. His eyes were a shade of light brown that glistened when light hit them, and his skin was a smooth chocolate. He was blessed with a succulent set of lips that left most women salivating.

It was good being the envy of men and the center of attention to women. Those benefits came along with being the saxophonist in MoJazz, a popular band that packed the house at a jazz club in downtown Jacksonville.

Maurice and his best friend and frat brother, Jamal Grover, had started the group when they attended Florida A&M University. They were currently working on independently releasing their first single, "Feel the Heat," a smooth slow jam that they felt was destined to become a hit.

Their genre of music was a unique blend of jazz, R&B, and spoken word, which provided an inimitable sound that would make waves in the music industry. Both Maurice and Jamal had been in the music game for quite some time, and they believed the group they'd put together was going all the way to the top.

Maurice stood and walked into the living area. He gazed around his condominium, looking at the mess that was made from last night's festivities. Empty bottles of Courvoisier, Hennessey, and Martell Cordon Bleu littered the floor. Half-empty plastic cups were everywhere. After MoJazz's performance at Encounters, he and a few friends brought the party back to his place.

The result was a night of lustful indulgence, a little too much to drink, and a visit from the sheriff's department for disturbing the peace. The gathering was broken up around three a.m., and everyone reluctantly headed home.

Living in upscale accommodations comprised mainly of retired neighbors, Maurice never had big parties because he was concerned that his rowdy friends would trash the place and disturb everyone. But after a few shots of Hennessey, he didn't have the ability to resist anything that showed the promise of pleasure.

I'd better clean this place before some unexpected company shows up at my door, he thought. Maurice went into the kitchen, grabbed a couple industrial-strength garbage bags, and went to work. After the quick cleanup, he sauntered back into his bedroom and opened the blinds.

Maurice noticed a piece of paper lying next to the alarm clock on the nightstand. It was a note from Kendra, the girl he'd met last night at the club. She'd spent the night in his arms but had left earlier in the morning.

Good morning, Mr. Sax Man,

Thanks for such a good evening. I usually don't do the one-night stand thang, but you were too irresistible and a sistah needed a little maintenance, if you know what I mean. It was all I hoped it would be! Sorry I couldn't hang around, but I do have a life to get back to. Take care!

Hugs & kisses,

Kendra

The imprint of her lips laced with bright red lipstick punctuated her signature.

Maurice suspected Kendra was married, and her goodbye note all but confirmed it. One of his unspoken rules was to never sex a married woman, but Kendra's long legs and luscious lips got the better of his judgment. Maurice shrugged his shoulders and balled up the note.

Enjoying and losing Kendra in one night didn't faze him. It was just another usual weekend of doing what he and Jamal did best--adding another name to their long lists of promiscuous encounters. There would surely be more willing and able Kendras.

Maurice figured he'd better hurry and get dressed. He was supposed to meet with his friend Simon at ten a.m. at Twilight for their standing Saturday visit.

While walking to the bathroom to begin his morning ritual, he heard moans and grunts echoing through the walls. His neighbors, the Hamptons, were indulging in their usual morning sex. Mrs. Hampton's sensual screams grew louder as she and her husband enjoyed a moment of physical intimacy. Well, at least Maurice assumed it was her husband.

Word on the street was that Mrs. Hampton had a thing for young black studs. She'd tried more than once to get Maurice to help her with a few things around the house-- when her husband was away, of course.

I really need to buy a house, Maurice thought as he turned on his Kenwood stereo and blasted the volume. The system came alive with the blissful tunes of Bilal's hit "Fast Lane." Maurice laughed at the irony of the song, which basically described the life he was living.

The fruits of success were always good to partake, but the nights of casual sex and the fast life were beginning to wear on his conscience. Since he was a mama's boy, he felt as if his mother was looking down on him from heaven and shaking her head. He began thinking about his mother and how much he missed her. He knew she would be disappointed with his lifestyle. He used the money that she left him in her insurance policy to buy all the trappings of the good life, but he was living foul.

5

She always told him, "Be careful what you wish for because not everything that looks good to you is necessarily good for you."

The pain of losing his mother was still a raw wound that stung his soul. Daisy LaSalle was a strong single mother who raised Maurice alone. But even Superwoman couldn't defeat the breast cancer that had taken her life four years ago.

Maurice wished that he could just go back to the old days when he was a youngster growing up in Alabama, running around without a care in the world. He and his friends would play games of tag and football, suck on Lemonheads and Red Hots, and chomp on Boston Baked Beans. He longed for the days when his momma would come out in the yard, yelling at him for fighting with the neighborhood kids or telling him that supper was ready.

His mother was a staunch Baptist, so she raised Maurice in the church with sound morals, which now provided him with a strong conviction and heavy conscience, even in the midst of his travels in the fast lane.

Maurice turned up the volume a bit more and jumped in the shower. Still exhausted after getting only three hours of sleep, he felt the aftereffects of the demanding sexual encounter with the voluptuous Kendra. The cool water provided a brisk awakening, invigorating his sore muscles and fatigued frame.

He heard the faint ring of the phone above the loud music. He stepped out of the shower dripping wet and picked up the cordless from the sink.

"Hello."

"What's up, fool?" Jamal said.

"Not much, player. Just getting out of the shower." Maurice dried himself with a nearby towel. "So tell me the blow-by-blow, pun intended, details with old girl you hooked up with last night."

"It was off the chain, bro. Let's just say ol' girl's got skills to pay the bills!" Jamal responded.

"She was all that, huh?" Maurice asked.

"Yeah, man. A brother was playing like a baby and sucking on those D cups all night. This chick was a total freak. She brought me back to her crib and it was on. She had a lot of sex toys in her closet."

Maurice chuckled. "Yep, that sounds like a freak all right."

"No doubt about that. But, yo, check this. We were upstairs in her bedroom getting our freak on and I was filleting that ass from the back when we heard a door downstairs slam shut," Jamal said.

"Aw shit!"

"Aw shit is right. It was her old man, bro! She said she wasn't expecting him until Sunday, but he showed up in the middle of the night. He must've suspected that he was being played."

"So what did you do?" Maurice asked, eagerly awaiting the reply.

"What the hell you think I did? I grabbed my shit and bailed out the window! I landed on some bushes and ran through the backyard like Carl Lewis. Man, I was putting on clothes and shoes in one motion." Jamal laughed.

"I told you about messing with married women."

"To top it off, the neighbor had a loud mouth Doberman barking his ass off. I hope they didn't see my black ass jumping from the second story window."

"Keep playing with that fire, my man, and you will get burned."

"Well, I got away in one piece. I hadn't had that much fun since you and I almost got busted at Linda's house."

They laughed in unison at Jamal's reference to an incident when they were teenagers; they'd snuck into a girl's home while her parents were asleep.

"Fun? That night wasn't fun at all, man. You bailed out the window while I had to hide under the bed when her father walked in," Maurice recalled.

"Damn, that brought back memories. Can't believe I'm still jumping outta windows at this age," Jamal reflected.

"That ought to tell you something," Maurice declared. "Well, my night wasn't as adventurous as yours, but it was aw'ight. After the cops broke up the party and you guys left, me and that chick who was sweating me had a little playtime of our own."

"So did you hit it?"

"You know I had to handle my business, man. I'm always looking forward to a meaningful one-night relationship."

"I hear that," Jamal replied.

"She woke up early this morning and split. She left a note thanking me for a good night."

"Man, this shit is just getting started. Wait until we go big time and get that national recognition. There'll be so much pussy falling from the sky, we'll need umbrellas and raincoats!" Jamal joked.

"Is that all you ever think about?"

"What'cha mean? Of course that's all I think about! You forget who you talking to?"

"Yeah, Mr. Trojan himself." Maurice had given Jamal the nickname Trojan because the amount of condoms he'd bought should've made him a spokesperson for the ever-reliable latex.

"So what are you getting into today?" Jamal asked.

"You know I volunteer at Twilight on Saturdays. I'll be there from ten to noon."

"Handle your business, sonny." Jamal laughed. "I'll holla at you tonight. You know it's ladies' night. It's gonna be thick with females up in there."

"Yeah, it should be blazing tonight. I'll see you in the dressing room later."

"All right. Holla back."

"One love." Maurice hung up the phone.

He was now running a bit late, so he hurriedly decided what to wear. Simon was from the old school and believed in looking your best at all times, so whenever Maurice went to visit he dressed sharp. Simon wouldn't settle for anything less and would give him a hard time if he came in there looking thuggish.

He opened his closet, which was laced with the best designer fashion in the business: Sean John, Versace, Prada, and Ralph Lauren, to name a few. Since he was in a flossing mood, he chose to sport a new outfit that had just hit the racks. He slipped into the black FUBU dress slacks and beige shirt, which outlined his muscular physique and was sure to make the ladies swoon as he made his way around town.

He slipped into a freshly shined pair of black Kenneth Cole leather loafers and took one last look in the mirror to make sure his appearance was on point. He grabbed his car keys and headed out the door.

He walked to the parking lot and pressed the unlock button on his key chain. The alarm disengaged his pride and joy: a brand-new platinum Audi TT Roadster that sported 18-inch chrome rims and customized everything. This elegant, panty-pulling machine was made for the purpose of commanding attention and, more importantly, attracting the opposite sex.

Maurice hopped in and gently cranked the ignition. The 225 horses under her hood began to gallop. He pressed a button on the driver's console and the convertible top retracted to its resting place. He then screeched out of the parking lot and headed for the interstate.

Maurice weaved from lane to lane on I-95, cruising 15 miles an hour above the speed limit. The traffic was minimal on Saturday since the working world was still sleeping late into the morning. His cell phone chirped above the sounds of wind and music. He answered, trying to pay attention to the road while opening the clamshell phone.

"Hello?"

"Hey, sweetie, how are you this morning?" Carmen's honey-covered voice filled his ears.

Carmen was one of his female *as*sociates. Maurice viewed his relationship with her as a mixture of platonic and romantic. Carmen lived only a few hours away in Orlando but would take time out to visit Jacksonville on occasion.

"Hello, Ms. Peaches," Maurice teased. He'd given her the nickname Peaches because he said she was so sweet and he really liked peaches. "I haven't heard from you in a while. How are things going?"

"I'm doing all right, Mo. Still going through all of the usual bullshit here in O'town," Carmen joked. "Why can't these fools just do right by a lady?"

"Still having man problems, huh?" Maurice asked.

"I don't know what I was thinking by trying to get back in the dating scene in this place. I think I'll just chill for a while. Besides, I like what you and I have going." Carmen not so subtly referred to her sexual rapport with Maurice.

They had it set up so they could spend time together whenever she was in town. The sex was good and, better yet, there were no strings attached. Both of them seemed quite content with that arrangement. Well, at least one of them did.

"Look, I have some business to tend to there in Jacksonville next week, and I need to see you," Carmen announced.

"That'll work. You know I'm always down for whatever," Maurice responded.

"That's much needed right about now. I'm feeling too lonely and horny these days and my fuzzy little peach needs some special attention."

"Well, you know how much I love to eat peaches."

Carmen laughed. "Boy, you so crazy! I'll give you a call tomorrow."

"Aw'ight then, Ms. Peaches."

"Just make sure you tell all your bitches not to disturb you while I'm in town."

"Aw, come on now. You know you're my one and only," Maurice lied.

"Tell that to someone who doesn't know the game. I better get back to work. I hate working on the weekend, but a sistah's got to handle business. Take care, Mandingo!"

"OK, Peaches, I'll eat you later. Oops, I mean, I'll see you later," Maurice joked.

"Men." Carmen shook her head and hung up the phone.

He smiled to himself at the thought of seeing Carmen again. It had been over two weeks since they enjoyed a *sexcapade*. Carmen was supposed to be a one-night stand, but she just didn't want to let go. Maurice didn't give much effort to resist her willingness to want to be with him. The sex was far too good to just let her go.

Carmen was a very attractive woman, and she had a body most men would die to touch, but looks weren't the only thing she had going. She was an intelligent, independent black woman who didn't take shit from anyone. Maurice really admired that about her.

Even though she was a beautiful, successful attorney, Carmen still had a bad side to her. She was paying back her two-timing ex-husband for cheating on her and breaking her heart. Or you could say that *he* was paying her back-- literally. She was taking him to the cleaners for every cent he had.

Maurice knew she could be a very vindictive person when provoked. But everything was going good, even though sometimes he wondered if he had stepped into a black widow's web by sexing a woman like Carmen.

Chapter Two

Ebony Eyes

Ebony Stanford leaned against the railing, admiring the view from the boardwalk. She was waiting for her cousin Monica, who she was meeting for brunch and drinks at a restaurant in Jacksonville Landing. Nestled along the St. Johns River in downtown Jacksonville and boasting a surplus of clothing outlets and themed eateries, The Landing was a popular hangout for everyone from corporate suits to hip-hop heads.

Ebony lifted her 35mm Minolta and began taking photos of a couple sharing a midday stroll along the boardwalk. Photography was her passion, and she never left home without her camera, just in case she came across the right moment for a frame. She had a keen eye, and she often brought out the best in a photo. Ebony captured the essence of romance as the couple held each other and shared a passionate kiss that seemed to last longer than the norm.

She could feel her heart tingle as she basked in the emotion of the moment. It was one of those days when she didn't want to be alone. Deep inside, that's exactly what she craved: companionship. Ebony wanted to feel the touch of love and experience its splendor once again, but she feared the burning twinge that accompanied a broken heart. It had been a long time since she was last touched in such a way. Her past was one of hurt and pain, and it was a challenge to move beyond. It was truly easier said than done.

The poisonous sting of divorce had cut through her heart like a searing blade through butter. Ebony and Bernard had been married only six months when she caught him cheating with another woman. He didn't even wait for the honeymoon period to end.

The painful memories consumed her as she remembered that terrible day that had altered her life. She'd gotten ill at work and decided to go home early. Bernard was supposed to be in New York on a business trip. He was an executive for a hot dot-com, and his job required a lot of traveling.

When she pulled up in her driveway, she was surprised to find her husband's Jaguar still parked at the house. She naïvely thought nothing of it. Sometimes his business trips were cancelled at the last minute. Ebony opened the door and walked into the three-bedroom house that she'd spent a lot of time and finances making into a home. She heard music coming from the stereo upstairs in the bedroom. She figured Bernard was in the shower with the music blasting as usual. The sultry voice of Teddy Pendergrass crooned his infamous hit, "Close the Door."

Her head was pounding from the migraine that was beating on her temple like a hateful stepmother. She went into the kitchen and took a few aspirin to relieve the pain and then proceeded upstairs to surprise Bernard. She opened the door to the master bedroom and noticed the bed was a mess. Her mouth hung open at the sight.

A red dress and black thongs lay at the edge of the bed, cheap patent leather pumps were on the floor, and gaudy earrings that weren't hers were next to the Tiffany lamp. The noxious smell of sweat, latex, and cheap perfume lingered throughout her bedroom. The French doors to the master bath were closed, and Ebony could hear water running in their forest green Jacuzzi with gold fixtures. It had taken her two months and trips to 20 different stores to get that bathroom the way she wanted it.

As she reached for the doorknob, she stepped on something that made a crackling noise. She looked down at the carpet and found an open condom packet. She nearly fainted as her mind raced a thousand miles per second. She heard a woman's voice on the other side of the door.

"Oh, Bernie! Fuck me harder, Bernie!"

Ebony flung open the French doors and there before her was her husband thrusting into a white woman bent over the rim of their Jacuzzi.

Tears filled Ebony's eyes, and her throat constricted. Everything seemed to flow in slow motion. Within seconds the hurt and shock was soon replaced by a ferocious anger.

"What the fuck is this?" Ebony yelled.

Bernard jumped at the sound of his wife's voice and stopped mid-stroke. His secretary screamed as she lost her balance and fell into the soapy water in the tub.

"Baby, I can explain!" Bernard's penis hung in front of him.

"I don't want to hear it! Both of you get the fuck out of my house!"

In a fit of rage Ebony ran out of the bedroom and headed downstairs. Her head hurt even more from the adrenaline pumping into her blood. With her mind racing beyond the speed of comprehension, she ran into the garage and opened the lockbox that was stashed away behind the washing machine. Ebony grabbed the .380 pistol from her lockbox and ran back into the house.

By the time she ran back upstairs, Bernard and his secretary had already made an exit. They both ran out of the house nearly naked, jumped in his car, and sped off.

After crying for what seemed like an eternity, Ebony took a deep breath and told herself that everything would be all right. But when she turned on the radio in the great room to help soothe her mood, the Shirley Murdock song "As We Lay" came on. Ebony snapped.

She took a Louisville Slugger to his Onkyo stereo and beat it down like it owed her something. She did a TaeBo kick to the Klipsch speakers, which went flying across the room and smashed into the bar, breaking a few bottles of his coveted Cristal.

Ebony ran into the bedroom and gathered all of her husband's clothes. She was in a hysterical daze as she walked out into the back yard and put his belongings into the barbecue pit. In a *Waiting to Exhale* moment, she doused everything with lighter fluid and threw in a match.

She then went into the living room and continued to obliterate the bar, which was her husband's pride and joy. After her rampage, she felt vindicated and smiled at all the damage she'd done. Since Bernard was such a materialistic person, she knew the best way to get him back was to utterly destroy everything he claimed was his.

Bernard tried calling her to apologize, but she didn't want to hear it. She'd put up with his shit long enough, and she just couldn't take it anymore. Ebony blamed herself for falling for the notion that she could change Bernard. After all, he was engaged to someone else when she met him.

She remembered her grandmother's words:

If you knew it was a scorpion when you picked it up, don't complain when it stings you because you knew what it was when you touched it.

After getting everything settled with the divorce, Ebony put all of her time and efforts into doing what she loved most: photography. She set off on her journey to pursue her goals and said to hell with men and the drama that came with them.

Ebony looked at her watch and noticed Monica was running late as usual. *Just like colored folk; we never show up on time.*

After Ebony received a hefty settlement, she decided to move to Jacksonville to be closer to her cousin. Ebony and Monica were born and raised in Louisiana, but Monica moved to Jacksonville a few years ago and was doing very well for herself as a marketing executive for a prominent bank in North Florida.

Monica was excited about Ebony joining her in Jacksonville, especially since she was newly single again. Monica thought they'd run the streets together for awhile and get Ebony back on track. But Ebony showed no interest in the dating scene.

It had been a year since she'd moved to Jacksonville, and Ebony had spent countless hours getting her business up and running. She opened a photo studio on the south side of town, which turned out to be an excellent location. Business was going well, and she was constantly booked for freelance projects from a variety of clients.

Ebony gazed at the big beautiful yachts lined up along the boardwalk, thinking how nice it would be to have one of those elegant boats to sail away on, forgetting all of her worries and traveling without a care in the world.

"I see you're still daydreaming as usual," a voice spoke from behind. It was Monica.

"What's up, cuz?" Ebony gave Monica a hug.

"Always something on that mind of yours, huh?"

"Just thinking about a few things, that's all." Ebony looked at her wristwatch. "It's about time you showed up. I've been sitting here for a half-hour waiting for you."

"I'm sorry, girl. I got tied up with Stacy. You know how she is once she gets to talking. Let's go inside and get a seat before the place gets crowded. I'm hungry as five big girls working through their lunch break."

Ebony picked up her camera bag, and they walked upstairs to the restaurant. Fat Tuesdays offered Cajun delicacies such as crawfish, red beans and rice, jambalaya, and the ever-famous gumbo. This was their favorite place to eat. Since both of them were from the bayous of Louisiana, this was the closest thing to home cooking they would get outside their kitchens. The place was packed with a variety of individuals, from college kids taking a break from studying to families enjoying the day.

"Damn, I should've thought of this idea," Monica said.

"What idea?" Ebony asked.

"I should've opened up a restaurant that was themed around Louisiana cooking. You know they can't throw it down like I can!" Monica beamed.

18

"That's not a bad idea. Who knows, maybe you should seriously look into doing something like that."

Looking like she'd tasted quite a bit of her own cooking, Monica was a healthy woman who teetered on the side of being overweight. But she didn't mind being overly thick in the right places; most men in the new millennium found it attractive.

They sat in the front of the restaurant near the window. Monica was checking out all of the fine fellas walking in. "Girl, I need to hook up with somebody tonight. I need my hair pulled and my ass slapped!"

Ebony's jaw dropped. "Look at you being all sluttish."

"I'm just keeping it real. It's been too long and you know a sistah's got needs. You should be able to relate. You haven't even been with a man since you moved down here."

Ebony frowned and gave Monica a look of contempt. "I'm not looking to get together with one either. Been there, done that; have the T-shirt and the scars," she laughed.

"Come on now. It's been almost two years now and you're still not over that shit yet? You're going to miss meeting someone nice if you keep this up," Monica scolded.

Ebony waved her hand dismissively. "I'm doing just fine being by myself. Bam Bam keeps me satisfied as long as I have an extra set of AA batteries. Besides, I don't need the drama from being in a relationship."

Monica laughed at her defensiveness. "If you say so, Ms. Dry Draws. But a sistah like me needs someone to put some satin in these panties. I gotta put some of this big girl luvin' on these fools." Monica playfully hoisted her breasts and arched her back.

19

A tall, handsome waiter approached the ladies as they began to get loose. "Hello, ladies, how are you this afternoon?" asked the Calvin Klein model look-alike.

Since Monica's hormones were already raging, she was the first to answer flirtatiously. "I'm doing fine Mr.?" Monica held out her hand.

He shook her hand. "Just call me Mike. I'll be your waiter."

"Oh, big Mike. I like that name. I'm Monica."

The waiter's cheeks turned crimson when he sensed the licentious intent in Monica's voice. He returned the smile and proceeded to take their order. "So what can I get you ladies?" he asked.

"I'd love a Screaming Orgasm for starters," Monica flirted.

Ebony tried to hold back her smile as she observed Monica trying to hit on the college-age stud.

Mike smiled and wrote down the order. He then looked over at Ebony. "And what about you, ma'am?" he asked.

"I'll take Sex on the Beach," Ebony answered. They always got a kick out of the ordering the popular drinks with sexual overtones.

Monica figured she'd just ask Mike a few personal questions. She wasn't interested in wasting time with chitchat. "Pardon my candor, but are you single?" Monica asked.

Mike licked his lips and smiled again. "Not exactly. I'm involved in a relationship with someone right now."

"She's one lucky woman," Monica said.

Mike put his hands on his waist. "Who said it was a woman?"

Ebony's eyes flew open, and Monica didn't miss a beat.

"Well, excuse me, Miss Thang!" Monica retorted.

"I'll be back with your drinks shortly." Mike expeditiously walked back toward the kitchen.

"Damn, Monica! Looks like you scared the poor guy."

Monica shook her head in disappointment. "How could someone that fine be as gay as a fruit loop? What a damn waste."

They both laughed. After a few moments of chatter, a young thug walked up to their table wearing a flea market Gucci outfit that was a few sizes too big. He had a bandana around his forehead that hung over one eye, and he was glittered down with fake diamond jewelry.

"S'up, ladies, my name is DeShawn. Y'all mind if a brotha has a seat?" He sat next to Ebony and put his arm around her before either could respond. Ebony looked over at Monica and grimaced. They'd gone from George Michael to Tupac.

"You got a little friend now, don't you," Monica joked to her cousin.

Ebony tried her best not to just fall out laughing as she looked at this hip-hop star wannabe trying to throw game her way. When he opened his mouth to speak, it looked like he'd just heisted Fort Knox. His entire grill was filled with gold-plated teeth.

"Actually, these seats are reserved. We're waiting for some friends," Ebony lied, trying to hold back a chuckle.

The young hip-hopster gave her an inquisitive look as he thought of a comeback response. "That's cool. I'll just lamp here 'til yo' friends arrive. Aw'ight?"

Ebony rolled her eyes with a bit of attitude. She looked over at Monica who was trying to hold back a laugh also. She grabbed his arm and politely moved it from around her neck.

"Sorry, but there will be no lamping here," Ebony said. "I think we'll be just fine, but thanks for the offer, DeShawn."

Realizing that he wasn't going to get anywhere, he tried to put on a hard act in order to save face. "Man, forget y'all stuck-up bitches," he shouted and pimp-strolled away.

Monica was just about ready to take off her earrings. "Oh no, he didn't!" She started to rise from her seat.

Ebony reached over and grabbed her by the arm. "Girl, don't even sweat it. He's just some ignorant ass who doesn't know how to respect a lady."

"He was about two seconds from a beat-down."

"See why I don't even go there with these fools," Ebony replied, shaking her head in disdain.

"Nigga damn near blinded me when he opened his grill. I don't know what's up with all of these fools thinking that if they're iced out with diamonds and gold that they'll attract a woman. The only thing they'll attract is some skank-ass hood rat."

Ebony leaned back and sighed. "They're just emulating what they see on television. Every time you turn on the TV there's some thugged-out fool surrounded by half-naked women shaking their asses in his face. These young kids are growing up seeing those images and want to be just like the man in the video."

"I guess. But damn, whatever happened to real men, to gentlemen? All you hear now is bitch this, ho that, and every degrading word you can think of to describe women," Monica said.

"No doubt about that. I can't wait until the day when I can find a true gentleman," Ebony agreed.

"You are preaching to the choir, cuz." Monica's cell phone rang. "Hold up a sec; lemme see who this is." Monica checked the caller ID display and flipped her phone open.

"Hey, Stacy. What you need now?"

"Hello to you too, ho," Stacy answered as she blew on her nail polish. "Hey, I forgot to ask you if you wanted to head out to Encounters tonight. It's ladies' night and we get in free before nine o'clock."

"Well, I'd planned on spending the evening with Ebony."

A few moments of silence passed after Ebony's name was mentioned. "Oh, I see." The hesitation in Stacy's voice was evident. She sighed loudly. "Well, why don't your bring her along?"

Monica was surprised that Stacy would suggest being in the same company with Ebony. "Hold on for a second," Monica replied. She turned to Ebony.

Ebony rolled her eyes when Monica looked her way.

"It's Stacy. She wants us to go to Encounters with her tonight. You up for it?"

Ebony looked out the corner of her eye. "You mean she wants *you* to go out with her."

"She just suggested we all go out. Come on, girl. It'll be fun!" Monica tried her best to sound sincere.

Ebony gave in to the look of amusement Monica had on her face. Since it had been such a long time, she figured maybe a night on the town was in order. She contemplated it for a few seconds.

"All right, but I'm doing this for you. You owe me one--make that 10."

"Oh please, this is for you. It's about time you get off that big ass of yours and shake it a little. You need to get laid so you can relax," Monica said.

Ebony waved off her sarcasm.

Monica picked up her phone. "Stacy? That sounds like a good idea. Where should we meet?"

"I'll just come over to your house around eight tonight," Stacy said.

"Cool. See you later then." Monica hung up the phone.

Ebony gave her an incredulous look. "You still hanging with Ms. Stuck-up?"

There was no love between Ebony and Stacy. She felt Stacy was far too snooty to hang out with common folk. She saw Stacy as a high-class bitch who used her God-given goods to get what she wanted. If it wasn't God-given, Stacy had no problems artificially enhancing it.

"I admit she does have an attitude problem and thinks that she's all that and a bucket of hot wings, but she's fun to be around," Monica replied.

"Well, you know how I feel about her, so we'll see just how much fun we have tonight."

"Whatever, girl. You guys need to get past that shit. She's my best friend, and you're my cousin."

"I know, I know. I can't help your poor judgment," Ebony retorted.

"Ha, ha, ha. You know I can't stand your girl Charlene, but you never hear me throwing it in your face every five minutes."

Ebony knew Monica was right, but she wasn't comfortable hanging around with Stacy. Her reputation spoke for itself and she couldn't understand why Monica even associated with her. Stacy slept with most of the top management at the bank. Her career advancement was achieved between the sheets with the higher-ups.

Ebony changed the subject. "So how's Aunt Shirley doing?"

"Mama thinks she's young again. She's got some new boyfriend who just moved in with her. She says he's a good man and he's taking care of her."

"Does she sound happy?" asked Ebony.

"Yeah, she sounds like she's in good spirits. I hope things stay that way."

"Least she's happy. That's what counts. You know how hard it is to find a good man these days."

Their waiter, Mike, returned with their drinks. "Here you go, ladies." He was acting more timid than the first encounter. "Is there anything else I can get you?"

Monica looked at him, then at Ebony, and back at him. "Trust me, Mike. You don't want to ask that question."

Mike smiled and once again made a quick exit.

Chapter Three

Strength, Courage and Wisdom

Maurice glided his silver macking machine into the Twilight Arms parking lot. Out of the corner of his eye, he noticed a beautiful figure walking toward him. It was Carla, a very fine nurse at the facility who gave all of the older guys a lift.

Damn, she must've been expecting me, he thought.

"Hey, Maurice!" Carla waved.

"What's up, Carla?"

"Not much, just doing my thang. So how are you this morning?" she asked, with a playful smile.

Carla had been trying to date Maurice for quite some time. Although she wasn't the prettiest woman, she sported a body that would have men paying for her to be the first choice at a bachelor party. Her 36-24-36 figure was the poster child for The Commodores hit song "Brick House."

Maurice didn't mind taking her out, but his schedule was already overbooked with women who were more than willing to partake of what he had to offer.

"I'm doing fine. How about you?" Maurice asked.

"I'm just keeping busy as usual with all of these dirty old farts," Carla answered. "I tell you, ever since they invented Viagra, that's all I ever hear about now. After all these years, I can't believe these guys are still occupied with getting their groove on."

Maurice laughed. "Some players never change, I guess."

"So is that what you are, Maurice? A player?" she questioned and gave him the don't-bullshit-me look.

"Nah, baby. I'm not a player, I'm just a coach," he replied jokingly.

She cracked a smile, which revealed her perfectly aligned pearly whites. "You're too much, Maurice."

"So where's Simon?"

"He's upstairs with the rest of the rowdy bunch."

"I'm a little late, so let me go holla at my boys."

Maurice turned to walk away, and Carla grabbed him by the arm. She gazed into his light brown eyes, and smiled once more. Her hand lingered on his bicep.

"You know, it's a good thing what you're doing by coming down here on Saturdays and spending time with these guys. It's not often that you meet brothers like yourself. I'm proud of you, Maurice."

"Hey, I'm just doing my thang. Besides, I learn a lot from these old-school cats."

Carla took advantage of the moment and hugged Maurice. She held onto him for a few seconds after he released his grasp. "I think you better get going," she finally said and stepped back.

"Yeah, let me go see what the guys are doing. Peace out, Carla." Maurice let her go and began to walk toward the building.

What was that about? He shook off the fleeting thought of the intense hug and went to the stairwell.

While walking up the stairs he could hear all of the commotion the guys were causing. *Just like black folk; always have to be the loudest,* he thought.

Maurice entered the lounge area and observed a comical scene unfolding. The group of guys was huddled around the table having their usual Saturday morning poker game. Today's topic of discussion was about the finest Black woman.

"You old-ass Negroes should know that Pam Grier is the finest of them all. Ain't nothin' like lookin' at that fine-ass sistah," yelled Clyde.

"I agree Pam is fine, but you gotta give it up for Beverly Johnson. Now that's one good-looking woman," Otis retorted.

"Man, y'all ought to get off those old broads," Simon chimed in. "They had their time, but now there's a new breed of females out there. Who's that big booty girl who played in that movie about the strip club?"

"You talkin' 'bout the one who played in *The Players Club.* She had a big ass, but she ain't no Pam Grier," Clyde yelled.

"Her name is LisaRaye," Maurice said, butting into their conversation.

The room momentarily filled with silence as everyone turned to see who had intruded upon their discussion.

Simon's eyes lit up when he saw Maurice. "MoJazz, what's up? Come on over here and give an old man a hug!"

Simon had given Maurice the nickname MoJazz and thought it fit him perfectly since he was a musician. Maurice liked the name so much that he chose to use it as the group's name. Maurice walked over and embraced the older man. The rest of the guys were happy to see Maurice. They all slapped dap and hugged before he took a seat at the card table.

"Hey, Mo, did you bring me that pack of Kools?" asked Otis, who looked like he'd smoked far too many cigarettes in his life.

Maurice pulled out the green and white box from his pants pocket and slid it over to him. "Don't tell anyone I gave you those," he said sternly.

"Boy, don't you know not to talk to your elders in that tone? I'll take this cane and pop you upside that peanut-shaped head of yours," Otis snapped.

"Otis, why you always tryin' to talk shit?" Clyde retorted. "Lookin' like the grim reaper is waitin' for your ass."

The entire room broke out in laughter.

"How's life been treating you, young buck?" Simon asked.

"Not too bad, man. Just taking it one day at a time."

"I hear that. That's all you can do; just take it day by day. Just make sure you use all those days wisely."

"So, Maurice, what kind of women you have this time? You have any pictures?" Clyde asked.

Otis turned to Maurice. "Forget the pictures; do you have some videos?"

Everyone nodded in agreement with Otis. They always wanted to hear the details of Maurice's sex life. Every now and then Maurice would give them the pleasure of enjoying a story or two. Each of them felt as if Maurice was living out their fantasies for them.

"Nah, fellas, I'm just lying low right now. Nothing much has been happening in the bedroom lately. I'm just busy concentrating on my music," he lied.

"Man, if I was your age I'd be tryin' to get all the pussy I could handle!"

"Otis, you know damn well ain't no woman gonna give you no play with your old shriveled-up balls," Clyde joked.

"Well, you can come over here and suck on these prunes, you old bastard. I'm sure you probably sucked on quite a few in your day, Mr. Happy," Otis retorted.

Everyone erupted in laughter. The guys always joked that Clyde, with his fine hair and pretty-boy look, must have been gay in his younger days.

"Fuck all y'all. I know I had me a lot of pussy in my days. Y'all just mad cause y'all didn't get as much as I did," Clyde snapped.

"MoJazz, I've heard enough of this. Let's head back to my room so we can talk," interrupted Simon. "Gotta get away from these old bags of dust before they have a bad influence on you."

"All right, Pops, let's roll." Maurice grabbed Simon's wheelchair, and they exited the lounge. Otis and Clyde were still ranking on each other about everything they could think of. Maurice and Simon conversed as they strolled down the corridor to Simon's room.

"So tell me what's up with you and Carla?" Simon asked.

"Huh? Me and Carla? Not a thing. We're just friends, old-timer. I'm not even trying to go there with her."

"Maybe you should re-evaluate the situation. She's a very nice woman."

Maurice knew where Simon was going with the conversation. He had been trying to get Carla and him together for a long time. "Yeah, she does seem like a nice girl, but you know me, Simon. That girl's looking for a husband, and I ain't the one."

"Well, you can't be out there running them streets forever, young blood. Life takes no prisoners in the game of love. Sooner or later you're gonna have to settle down and find that one special person. Take it from me, you don't want to be all lonely and by yourself when you get older. That's the beauty of having that one special woman in your life. Someone you can grow old with. You feel me, homie?" Simon attempted to sound hip.

Maurice smiled as Simon dropped some knowledge. "Yeah, man, I feel you."

"I'm serious, MoJazz," Simon continued. "You're 32 years old, and you're a good man. You know there are a lot of beautiful black queens out there looking for a strong black king. Time's come to stop thinking with that wayward dick of yours and start really thinking about settling down."

As much as he didn't want to hear it, Maurice knew Simon was right. He was much closer to being old than he was young. He was just afraid of the commitment thang. He'd seen it hurt more people than help.

"I don't know if the family thang is for me. I've seen so many couples doing fine until the M-word was introduced. Then everything just seemed to change. Besides, who could expect a marriage to last in this day and time? The divorce rate is climbing, and I'm not looking to become another statistic."

"Count your blessings, young brother. There are many people who'd love to be in your shoes. Trust me; life could always be worse, so be thankful and quit complaining so much."

"True dat." Maurice nodded his head in agreement.

"We need young brothers like you to carry on the new black generation. All I see when I watch television is a culture obsessed with sex, money, and materialism. It's destroying us, man." Simon was on his soapbox. "Don't get me wrong, I love to see young blacks getting ahead, but we're destroying the fabric of our culture just to get there.

"I remember back in the days when the black woman was cherished. Now all I hear are these fools calling them hoes and bitches, then the same fools turn around and say they love their mother and get up there thanking God at awards shows. Most of these young cats don't even know what the struggle was about. They probably don't even care."

This was an issue that always made Simon upset. He couldn't stand to see black folk stepping on and disrespecting each other just to reach their goals. Simon was truly a fighter in his day and wanted to see a younger generation of fighters for the black community that could continue that legacy. He decided to change the subject before his blood pressure went skyrocketing again.

"How's your music coming along, MoJazz?" Simon asked.

"We're still laying down some final tracks for our single. It's going to be a big hit. I'll make sure you're at the release party."

"Thanks, I'll be sure to clear my calendar for that night." Simon laughed heartily. "I'm proud of you, kid. You're gonna make it big."

"I'm damn sure trying to."

"Well, you know I can still teach you a thing or two on the keys." Simon winked at Maurice.

"You're the master. I'm just the apprentice trying to take in as much as I can."

A very talented pianist, Simon could've easily become one of the jazz legends of his time. Very few had the melodic dexterity that he possessed. But his association with the wrong people in the music industry nearly cost him his life. Thanks to a gunshot wound, he was confined to a wheelchair for the remainder of his time in this world. He was determined to not let Maurice travel the road he once walked.

"There's just too much of this technology in music today. Whatever happened to the pure sound of instruments? You know-- the soul of music."

"I hear ya. That's what we're trying to bring back," Maurice replied.

"I think it's robbing the pure creative musicians from their coveted positions of being true creators. All these producers are doing now is sampling old songs."

"There's no denying that, but you have to admit that's still creative."

Simon dismissed Maurice's comment with a wave of his hand. "These young cats don't have any appreciation for the craft of music. To them, it's about that bling-bling lifestyle instead of a love for the craft. You don't hear that pure soul music anymore."

"Well, my love for the craft runs deep, and I'll try not to get caught up in the bling-bling lifestyle." Maurice laughed.

"Take it from me, young blood. That's a path you don't want to take. You see where it got me." Simon patted his wheelchair.

"I won't, Pops. I'll stay grounded and keep it real."

Simon sat back with a smile that a proud father would give to a son. That's exactly the way he saw Maurice--as the son he never had. He recognized the talent and gift that Maurice possessed, which reminded him of himself when he was young. He didn't want Maurice to make the mistakes he did.

"Just don't give up, MoJazz. One of the most important things you must learn is perseverance. It overcomes everything there is. Just never stop trying."

Maurice listened intently to the advice of his dear friend; he was filled with respect and admiration for the old man.

"The Bible says without a vision the people perish. Keep focused on your vision, young blood, and never, ever give up."

"I'll always remember that, Simon," Maurice replied, a smile forming at the corner of his lips.

A loud knock at the door refocused their attention.

"Simon, bring that snotty-nosed youngster out here so we can whip his ass in a game of spades," Otis yelled through the closed door.

"All right, you old wet sack of nickels; hold your horses," Simon responded then turned to Maurice. "Just remember one thing, MoJazz. Nothing in life is free. Everything has a price, and you must give up something to get it. The greater the value, the greater the sacrifice. Just make sure you're willing to pay that price."

"Have you always been this deep, old man?"

"Let's just say I've experienced enough shit to last a lifetime. Being out on the streets taught me a tough lesson about life."

"Like what?"

"In life there's only two types of people--the one's who are pimping and the one's who are being pimped. If you don't know which one you are then you're the ho. Remember that."

Chapter Four
Bad Boy For Life

Jamal stood butt naked, looking at himself in the mirror. He flexed, striking a double bicep pose. At 6 feet 3 inches and with 230 pounds of solid muscle, Jamal was a sight to behold, and he knew it.

"Damn, you look good. You go boy!" he boasted.

His girlfriend, Nicole, sat on the bed in her birthday suit, frowning as she gave him a look of disdain. "You're too stuck on yourself, Jamal."

"Woman, you know you love this fine piece of meat right here." Jamal grabbed all nine and a half inches of his manhood.

They'd just finished making love or, better yet, they'd just finished having sex. Nicole was the only one who felt she was making love when they lay together. To Jamal, she was just another piece added to his list.

Nicole shook her head. She couldn't deny that Jamal had whipped some type of love spell across her sense of logic. No matter how many times she tried to leave, she just couldn't.

She and Jamal had been sexual partners for a year, and she mistakenly had the notion that she could change him. Even though she knew that he was the worst type of man, her heart still longed to be with him. She was often left hating herself for clinging to such a false sense of hope.

"If you don't keep that piece of meat in your pants, it's gonna fall off," Nicole retorted.

Jamal frowned. "There you go making dick threats again."

"I'm not making any dick threats. I'm just saying that you need to realize what you have right here. Why you gotta go run around with all those hoochie mamas out there?"

Jamal didn't want to hear any lectures about his promiscuous behavior. He was becoming aggravated with the direction the conversation was taking. He knew once Nicole started talking, she wouldn't let up. She'd keep going and going like the Energizer Bunny.

"Look, I'm not in the mood to be fussing today." He turned away and left the room. Jamal walked into the kitchen and opened the refrigerator. He grabbed a Bud Light and popped the cap. Nicole came storming into the kitchen and slammed the refrigerator door shut.

"You still didn't tell me where you were last night," she continued. "I tried calling your cell and your home phone and got no answer."

Jamal rolled his eyes, waved his hand, and took a swig of his ice-cold brew.

"So you keeping tabs on me?" he asked.

"No, I'm not keeping tabs on you. I'm just worried about you."

"Worried about me?" he asked. "I'm a grown-ass man. You don't have to worry about me."

Nicole was so pissed off that she drew back and knocked the beer out of Jamal's hand. Bud Light went flying across the kitchen onto the counter and floor.

"See, that's what I'm talking about, Jamal. Your ass is so conceited that you can't even see past your dick."

"What the fuck is wrong with you? Try that shit again and you'll be picking your jaw up from the floor!" Jamal snapped.

Nicole shook her head. "How could you be so selfish?" she asked. "Did you ever stop to think about me?"

Jamal gave her a puzzled look. "What about you?"

Nicole closed her eyes and prayed for God to give her the strength to keep from hurting this man. "Jumping around from woman to woman is going catch up with you one of these days," she screamed.

"Well, you know me. I just can't have one piece of pussy in my life. It's always been like that. My daddy did it, my grandfather did it, and, hell, my great grandfather was the biggest pimp in Chicago. Matter of fact, we was probably pimpin' on the plantation. It's in my blood. I'm a Grover man. You better recognize." Jamal pimp-walked back into the bedroom.

Nicole followed right behind him, stride for stride. "That's the sorriest excuse I've ever heard. You're nothing but a dog, Jamal." She punched him on the arm.

Jamal did a double bicep pose again and flexed his arms. "You got that right, baby. A dog and proud of it!" he replied, pointing to the Omega brand on his upper arm. "Q-Dog for life, baby! Omega Psi Phi!"

Nicole turned her nose up and stormed past him. She walked into the master bathroom and slammed the door. She wasn't sure how much more she could take. Her mind was telling her to kick his sorry ass out of her house. But her heart was telling her to hold on, that he'll change.

Jamal banged on the bathroom door. "Hurry up in there, woman! I got things to do today!"

Nicole stood looking at herself in the mirror above the sink. *How did I get here? Am I that damn desperate?* she wondered. After sacrificing to put herself through college and survive all on her own, how had she come to this point?

"Last I checked I still pay the bills in this motherfucker! I'll come out when I damn well please!"

Jamal walked over to the bed, picked up his clothes, and got dressed. He didn't have time to sit there and listen to Nicole bitch and moan. He had more important things on his agenda, including visiting another one of his *asso*ciates. Without saying another word, he got dressed and walked out the door.

Nicole's eyes were red and misty. She looked in the mirror and shook her head at what she saw. After hearing the door shut, she walked out of the bathroom. The scent of sex still lingered throughout her apartment. Nicole sat at the edge of the bed of crumpled sheets, put her hands in her face, and began to sob.

Jamal cruised down I-295 in his customized Lincoln Navigator. He didn't want for anything when it came to material possessions. His bedroom talent paid off for him after an old rich woman he used to service passed away. She included him in her will. He never did tell his partners how much money he got, but he had cash to spare and a nice house out near the beach.

He was on his way to the west side of Jacksonville to visit Chantel. Jamal loved the excitement of living dangerously and so did Chantel. She was an unhappily married woman with two children. Her husband was in the Marines and stationed at the Jacksonville Naval Air Station. Since he spent so much time away from home, she had just the opportunity she needed to get away from her mundane lifestyle.

Jamal picked up his cell phone and dialed Chantel's number. His number was restricted from showing on caller ID just in case her husband answered the phone. If need be, he would disguise his voice and play the role of telemarketer.

"Hello?" Chantel answered.

"Is your bodyguard around?" Jamal asked.

"Nah, he's in the field and won't be back until tomorrow afternoon!" she replied excitingly.

"That's good. So is little Nina ready to play?" Jamal teased. He'd nicknamed her vagina Nina, the street name for a nine-millimeter pistol. He always joked that she had some dangerous love.

"Daddy, I've been thinking 'bout riding that pony of yours all week. It's quiet over here; the kids are over at my sisters."

Jamal smiled at the thought of sexing Chantel. He wasn't sure what kind of sensuous delight she had in store for him this time.

"Well, I can't wait to smack that ass of yours," he teased.

"Hurry up, I'm wet with anticipation," she shot back.

"Aw'ight then, I'll be there in a few minutes." Jamal hung up the phone and stepped on the gas. He had an insatiable sexual appetite. In just a few hours he'd sexed a married freak and reached the peak of passion with Nicole. Now it was time for another run.

Jamal parked his truck around the corner a few houses down from Chantel's place. He reached into his glove compartment and pulled out a pair of edible thongs he'd bought at Romance Emporium.

He then walked briskly up to Chantel's door and rang the doorbell to her townhouse. After a few seconds, Chantel opened the door. Jamal was silenced into submission once he took a look at her. She was wearing a long see-through black lace gown. Her braided hair was pulled back and tied into a ponytail.

Jamal's eyes quickly glanced up and down, admiring her sexy appearance. Chantel's partially exposed breasts peered from behind the lace, screaming for attention. The stilettos she wore caused her calves to flex, adding more sex appeal to her already dime-piece figure.

"Damn, I'm happy to see you." Chantel cooed.

Jamal walked in and closed the door. "We're happy to see you too." He grabbed his crotch.

Chantel didn't waste time. She rushed to Jamal and put her hand on top of his. They began a long and passionate kiss.

"I need you, darling. I need you inside of me right now!" she demanded.

"I'm all yours, but first I need to go take a shower."

"You've still got the scent of another bitch on you, huh? All right, take a shower, but make it fast!"

Jamal went into the master bath and turned on the shower. While he was busy getting scrubbed down, Chantel began preparing for some sexercise. She lit aromatherapy candles to help set the scene. She then went over to the stereo and put in her old Silk CD. The sensuous tunes of Silk's hit song "Freak Me" echoed throughout the room.

The choice of music reflected her mood. She wanted Jamal to know that she wanted to fuck.

"Jamal, hurry up, damn it! I'm horny as hell!" Chantel demanded.

She lay in her bed impatiently waiting for her lover to emerge from the bathroom. Looking incredibly stunning, the black negligee she wore contrasted perfectly with the white satin sheets she lay upon. It provided one hell of a visual and looked like a perfect spread for the pages of *Playboy*.

Jamal opened the bathroom door and walked into the bedroom. Chantel admired his six-pack abs, which were tight enough to bounce a quarter on. His cornrowed hair provided the thug appeal that she relished. She felt as if she were the good girl who had finally gotten her bad boy.

"Come here, daddy." Chantel curled her finger and beckoned him to her. She raised herself on all fours and waited at the edge of the bed. Jamal approached her with his hardened penis in his left hand and a Trojan in his right.

"Let's get this party started." Jamal mischievously grinned.

Chantel grabbed his dick and took it whole into her mouth. She began sucking him slowly, taking in as much as she could. The taste of him was intoxicating to all of her senses. She increased her pace as she continued applying her skilled oral technique. Chantel soon released his dick from her mouth and lay back on her bed. She wanted his thick, hot jimmy inside of her.

Jamal put on his condom then followed her cue. Their bodies blended together. When he entered her, Chantel let out a gasp.

"Right there, daddy! Right there!"

Jamal proceeded to put the remaining portion of his manhood inside her. Chantel immediately began trembling. Her wetness soaked the sheets. Jamal rammed into her with full force, applying long deep strokes.

Chantel began squealing in a high pitch. "Oh...oh...oh...ah!" she wailed, her nails digging deeply into his back.

Jamal's deep thrusts were met with Chantel's pelvic rotations. Within minutes, Jamal withdrew and turned Chantel over. Now she was in his favorite position: doggy style.

"Bow wow wow, yippee yo yippee yay!" he chanted while throwing up the Q-dog sign.

Chantel's beautiful caramel-colored ass looked so inviting. Her pleasure center was dripping with moisture. Jamal didn't waste any time as he slid his long shaft into her from behind.

Chantel's pear-shaped ass slapped up against his lower abdomen. The slapping sound of skin on skin turned him on even more. He began to increase the speed of his strokes. His large hands wrapped around her petite waist, holding on to her as he sexed her from behind. Chantel screamed and moaned as she gripped the edge of the bed.

She could feel the throbbing sensation of his dick as it rapidly moved in and out of her.

After 20 minutes of the most intense sex Chantel had experienced since their last encounter, she began to quiver. Jamal could tell that she was approaching climax. He grabbed her ankles and maneuvered her into the wheelbarrow position. Chantel felt as if her body was about to explode when he reached her innermost parts. Her toes curled, and her eyes rolled back into her head until only the white part was showing. Within seconds she screamed and let out an intense orgasm that felt like an earthquake had just hit North Florida.

Jamal's muscles began to tense. The slapping sound of their skin was now loud enough to wake the neighbors. With each thrust, Jamal could feel his semen beginning to shoot forward. Just as he was about to come, he withdrew, pulled off his condom, and shot his load all over Chantel's back. He continued to jerk and spasm as the aftereffects of ejaculation set in. They both collapsed onto the bed and lay motionless next to each other, exhausted.

Chapter Five
Hot In Here

Maurice arrived at Encounters at eight p.m. sharp. The line already stretched around the corner of the building, and the parking lot looked like a Cash Money Records car show. The tightest cars and the tightest females in the city were on display for ladies' night.

A variety of attractive women stood in line, anxious to get their groove on and partake of the evening's festivities. They were dressed in everything from business suits to tight miniskirts. The brothas were sporting everything from the latest sweat suits to designer suits. Everyone looked as if they'd made the beauty salons and barbershops rich that day. It was all one big show.

The old warehouse had been turned into the hottest spot in town after sunset, especially on the weekend. Encounters was a one-stop entertainment venue that boasted three levels of amusement. It contained a classy soul food restaurant, a sultry jazz club, and a high-tech disco. It was the perfect haven for children of the night.

In the jazz section, where MoJazz performed, the evenings usually began with a poetry slam as writers and poets performed their latest work. On weekdays, Encounters hosted comedy sessions by well-known and up-and-coming comedians. Talent scouts sometimes lurked in the audience hoping to discover the next *Comic View* all-stars.

The disco on the top level attracted a much younger crowd who grooved to the tunes of the latest hip-hop stars. Players, ballers, and players and ballers on a budget were all over the place.

Maurice pulled his roadster up to the side entrance gate and beeped his horn. A burly man with short dreadlocks who looked like he just did a prison bid approached the car. It was Darren, one of the club's bouncers. Everyone called him Big D.

"What up, Maurice?" Darren asked.

Maurice stepped out of his car looking debonair. A tailored, five-button burgundy pinstriped Armani suit hugged his frame.

"Not much, Big D. Just running a bit behind. Looks like you have a packed house tonight."

"You know it's ladies' night, so this place is gon' be packed. I'm sure most of them are here to listen to you guys play. I just hope none of these fools start trippin' tonight."

"Don't sweat it. Once they take a good look at a brotha as big as you, there won't be any beef."

"You best believe I'll keep it in check, though," Darren replied.

"Thanks for looking out for my baby. Make sure you park her in a good spot." Maurice slid him the keys and a tip. "Another thing, Big D, when we become famous I'll make sure you're on our security team."

Big D smiled. "I'm yo' man, Mo. That'll work; thanks for lookin' out."

Maurice walked around to the back entrance of the club, which led straight to the dressing rooms. The line outside seemed to grow by the minute. Maurice smiled because he knew it was sure to be off the chain tonight.

The rest of the band was in the dressing room *chillaxin* before their first set. Jamal was in the corner going over his vocal runs, making sure his heart-melting voice was ready to work its magic. Chauncey, the bass player, was going through his pre-show meditation ritual. Ever since his trip to Thailand, he'd come back talking about Buddhism and the power of meditation. He freaked everyone out, but as long as he continued to funk up the place with the bass, it was all good.

Devon, also known as Baby Fingers, was on the keyboards, and Michael held down the percussion. They were playing a last-minute game of dominoes.

Each band member was an exceptional musician in his own right. Everyone played more than one instrument and would change positions during their show just to show a bit of versatility.

When Maurice opened the door of the dressing room, he was greeted by the pleasant sounds of The Phat Cat Players CD. Their hit tune "Sundress" echoed as Coco Brown's baritone voice set the mood. Maurice sat his saxophone case down.

"What's up, fellas? Sorry I'm running a bit late."

"What's up, Mo?" Jamal asked. "Looks like it's gonna be off the heezy tonight! Time to give the honeys what they came for."

"Just don't get carried away, Mr. Lover!" Devon laughed.

"Y'all see all those fine females waiting in line?" Chauncey asked.

"We need to tell Greg to start thinking about increasing our salary. This has to be the eighth week straight that we've packed the joint!" Devon griped.

"Don't worry about that, Baby Fingers. Now y'all know I've always made sure everyone here gets paid, right? So I'll have a little meeting with Greg to make sure we get our piece of the pie," Maurice said.

Ever since the group was hired as the live entertainment for Encounters, the crowd had nearly doubled. Business was booming as the word got out about this local band that was tearing up the spot. The buzz had become so strong that it even attracted attention from some major labels, who'd sent people to sit in on a couple of sets.

It was close to show time. Maurice led MoJazz in their pre-show prayer to get them pumped up. The guys left the dressing room and headed backstage, where they ran into Greg, the club owner.

"Hey, Maurice. What's up, my man?" Greg asked.

"Hey, G-man. How's it hanging?" Maurice replied, as they gave the brother-to-brother embrace.

"I can't complain, man. Look at all this." Greg said, referring to the size of the crowd. "I hope we don't get a visit from the fire marshal tonight. This place is damn near over capacity."

"Business is booming." Maurice nodded.

"It sure is, man. You guys just keep throwing down that magic! People are coming back with their friends. The word is getting out."

"That's just what we need before our single drops. That should help to bring in even more fans."

"My man! That's what I'm talking about! A brother who thinks ahead."

Maurice leaned in to emphasize the point he was about to make. "Just make sure we get our piece of the pie."

"You know I'm gonna look out for a brother. Your band is the main draw. Trust me, I'll do whatever I can to make you happy as long as y'all keep the fans coming back for more.

"No doubt, we'll keep the ladies wet; that you can bet." Maurice dapped up Greg, and they parted ways.

Maurice walked to the backstage area as the rest of the band members took their positions. The DJ reduced the volume on Boney James' single "Ride." Greg walked from behind the curtains and surveyed the crowd. The jazz room was colored in shades of red and filled with cocktail tables. Each table had a single rose and a lit candle in the center.

The chatter of the filled room subsided as everyone turned their attention to the stage. Greg paused for a second and did a Temptations-style spin with his head down. Then he looked up and grabbed the microphone.

A lady in the front shouted out, "You go, boy!"

"Welcome, ladies and gentlemen, but especially ladies. I would like to thank everyone for coming out tonight and showing so much love. It's good to see so many good-looking black folks."

A man shouted, "Damn, you got that right!"

Greg continued his introduction. "I have a special treat in store for you tonight. I know you've been waiting to hear them, and the time has arrived to bring you the funk! This band has traveled across the land, laying down the funkiest sounds around. So without further ado, I'd like to introduce you to the best band in the land! Give it up for Jacksonville's own, MoJazz!"

The club erupted with thunderous applause as the curtains opened. Michael tapped the drumsticks for the opening count. After the fourth hit of the drumsticks, the rest of the instruments came to life. Chauncey lit up the bass, and everyone followed. Their opening selection was "Ascension," the hit tune by Maxwell.

The spotlight focused on Jamal as he slowly faded in with his sultry vocals. The ladies went crazy when Jamal spit out those blissful notes, just as good as Maxwell himself. Maurice stepped into the spotlight next to Jamal with his tenor saxophone. The audience applauded as Maurice played in tune with Jamal's voice. The harmony between the tenor sax and Jamal's voice was hypnotic.

Maurice went into a full solo with his gleaming brass saxophone. He blew his very life into the mouthpiece as the instrument spewed out melodic tunes. He fed from the energy the crowd was giving him. He closed his eyes and entered into his flow.

"Damn, that boy can play!" a voice yelled.

After a few moments passed, Maurice opened his eyes and peered into the audience. He was hoping to find another participant for a night of passion and dirty tricks. The place was packed, and the crowd swayed to the rhythm emitted from the stage. A few ladies made their way up front.

"I paid my money to see some skin!" a drunken woman screamed.

Jamal was more than willing to give her a personal show. He walked to the edge of the stage and began to do pelvic gyrations while singing in her direction. A younger lady stood next to the intoxicated woman, holding her arm. The look on her face displayed her embarrassment. Maurice smiled at them and continued playing.

While Maurice scanned the crowd, his eyes rested upon the most beautiful vision of loveliness in the room. She was sitting in the center of the room, a few tables from the bar. Her beauty nearly interrupted his flow as they made eye contact and entered into an intricate dance of sensual attraction.

Dressed in a red dress with spaghetti straps, her beauty was stunning. She stood out from all of the other women in the club. Maurice couldn't take his eyes off of her as he continued to play his solo.

He winked, and she smiled in return. He knew he'd gotten her attention because she was blushing and couldn't keep her eyes off of him. After a minute she turned to her girlfriends, and they all began giggling. Maurice finished his solo and stepped out of the spotlight.

Jamal came in with a vocal run that sounded like a mix of Aaron Hall and Stevie Wonder. Jamal then unbuttoned his shirt to his rippled stomach, and the ladies in the front row hooted and hollered. This was Jamal's environment, and he loved every second of the attention.

"It's about damn time! That's what I wanna see!" the drunken woman slurred.

Maurice looked at Baby Fingers on the keys. They smiled at the way the younger woman had to hold back her mother.

Jamal took off his shirt and threw it in the direction of a few other females who had congregated at the front of the stage. He began to do more gyrations and pelvic thrusts as more women made their way to the stage. The scene was beginning to transform from a laid back jazz club to a Chocolate Express strip show. Women were reaching into their purses pulling out dollar bills, begging for Jamal to come closer.

"Take it all off!" one woman shouted.

In the midst of the ruckus, a thong found its way onto the stage. After a few moments of Jamal's showboating, Maurice figured he better give the cue to end the song before things got too out of hand and turned into a 2 Live Crew show. Maurice knew Jamal could go overboard when given the opportunity. Before you knew it, he'd be running around onstage in his birthday suit.

Maurice raised his hand, and everyone followed through as Jamal ended the song with a run that left the audience screaming for more. A few women continue to wave dollars in the air.

Michael then took center stage and began to entertain the crowd with a little poetry that he'd written. While Michael put on a brief slam, Maurice leaned over to Devon.

"Man, you see that sweetness over in the red dress?"

They both looked at each other and sang, "My, my, my" in harmony.

"That's what I call fine!" Maurice said.

"Damn, she is fine," Devon replied.

"I gotta holla at her after we finish."

"Do your thang, player."

The woman in the red dress sat at a table with two other females. They were laughing and seemed to be having a good time. From time to time, she'd glance at Maurice and make eye contact. Every time she smiled, it sent tingles up and down his spine. He just had to meet this breathtaking woman.

After a pause for the cause of poetic expression, the band returned to the stage to finish out their set. The audience swayed and grooved to the band's hypnotic tunes. After the last song, everyone stood and applauded.

Maurice grabbed the mic. "I hope you enjoyed our first set. Stick around for our second set. We have a special treat in store for you."

The curtains closed and the guys dapped each other on such a bad-ass performance. Jamal ran backstage to get another shirt. Greg ran from the side of the stage.

"Man, that was one hell of a set! Just wait until the second set, when you-know-who shows up." He dapped the rest of the crew.

"Is he here yet?" Devon asked.

"Yeah, he just got in. He's back in the dressing room," Greg said.

Maurice had his mind on one thing: getting out front so he could meet the sweetness in the red dress.

"All right, guys, let's meet back here in 20. I gotta do some mingling."

"Uh oh, looks like lover boy done seen something that's caught his eye," Chauncey laughed.

Jamal walked over next to them. "I saw something that caught my eye as well."

"Better not be my woman you're talking 'bout. Did you see ol' girl in that red dress?" Maurice asked.

"Yeah, I saw her, but did you see the one sitting next to her with the halter top?"

"Nah, I was just hooked on the red dress."

"Then what the hell we doing talking to each other back here? Let's go holla!"

Both Maurice and Jamal rushed off the stage so they could make their way to the table where the intriguing ladies sat. When they entered the lounge they noticed the ladies were still seated at their table, laughing and enjoying themselves.

Jamal was nearly run down when he appeared in the crowd. Grown ladies were acting like young girls at a B2K concert.

"Jamal, here's my number!" yelled one lady, sliding a slip of paper into his pants pocket.

Another beautiful woman whispered in his ear. "I threw that black thong on stage for you. If you want to see what's under this dress, come by my place tonight."

Jamal looked into her eyes, leaned over, and whispered, "Thank you very much, but I'm taken."

The lady accepted his rejection without getting ignorant and was just as happy that he noticed her.

Both guys kept smiling and shaking hands as they made their way over to the table where the ladies were.

Monica noticed that the guys from the band were heading their way. "Girlfriends, looks like the spotlight is on us."

"Damn, they're hella fine!" Stacy yelled, making no attempt at being cool.

"You got that right!" Monica concurred. "Ebony, here comes that saxophone player you were talking about."

Ebony tried to play the nonchalant role. "Girl, please! You know I don't have time for these fools up in here."

"You're going to miss meeting someone nice if you keep this up. Besides, these guys are semi-famous. You know what that means? Cha-ching, girlfriend!" Stacy slapped five with Monica.

Ebony smirked but didn't say what was on her mind. *Yeah, you're just like all the rest of the groupies. Nothing but a trick who'd lay down with anything who threw dollars her way,* Ebony thought.

"This could be your chance. You know it's been a while since you've been with a man," Monica said.

"I told you before, I'm not looking to hook up with anyone," Ebony retorted. "I just don't want to get involved with another man right now. Even if it were like that, why would I want to get with a musician? You know the type of lifestyle they live."

"I'm not saying you have to marry the man. There's nothing wrong with getting a little diggidy every now and then. Look at them. You see them giving us the eye, and they're some handsome brothas," Stacy scolded.

Ebony just sat back and didn't say another word. She sipped from her glass of Alizé.

"Here they come," Monica said softly.

Ebony looked up, and her eyes met with Maurice once again. The closer he moved toward her the more she could feel her heart pounding. She squirmed as she tried to reposition herself in the chair and sit up properly. Jamal and Maurice walked right up to their table.

"Excuse us, ladies. We don't mean to intrude, but we just couldn't help but notice the finest women in the room," Jamal said.

"Can we buy you lovely ladies a drink?" Maurice asked, never taking his eyes from Ebony.

"Yes, of course! Please have a seat," Stacy replied excitedly.

Who appointed this bitch group leader? Ebony thought. She smiled while Maurice pulled up a chair and sat next to her.

"I'm Jamal, and this is my best friend, Maurice." They shook hands and began sizing each other up.

Stacy couldn't resist feeling like a little girl once she heard the sound of Jamal's deep, seductive voice. She was mesmerized when he was singing; now she experienced his charm up close and personal. He was the perfect physical specimen for her.

If his dick is half the size of his shoes, then Lawd have mercy, she thought. Stacy's eyes kept drifting downward toward his crotch as they began to converse.

"Ebony. That's a lovely name." Maurice gazed into her eyes.

Ebony's attraction to him made her really nervous. She adored his light-brown eyes and considered complimenting him but figured every woman he met probably did. *Get yourself together, girl*, she thought.

"Thanks," she replied.

Ebony glanced at Stacy and Jamal, who were already in their own little world and had blocked out the conversation the others were having. Stacy was star struck and her eyes were glossed over, which meant by the end of the night Jamal would have her cute French-manicured toes reaching for the sky.

"So what's it like having all these women throw themselves at you?" Ebony smiled coyly.

"It's all good. What can I say? We appreciate the love from our fans."

Yeah, right! I'm sure you appreciate much more than that, she thought.

"I really enjoyed the show. You have skills with the sax."

Maurice smiled and gave her another wink. "Well, I try my best."

Damn, I sound like a clown, he thought. This was the first time a woman made him lost for words. This feeling was bizarre for him since he was quite the ladies' man. A few moments of silence passed.

"How long have you been playing?" Ebony asked.

"Ever since I was 10 years old. I started in grade school and just couldn't put the damn thing down. While all the other kids were playing outside, I was stuck in my room taking music lessons. But I guess it has paid off so far."

Ebony took another sip from her glass as she tried to calm herself and not show any signs of excitement. Both of them seemed a little uneasy in each other's presence. The vibes of attraction were undeniably thick. They talked for a while until Maurice noticed that it was time to get ready for their second set. Both he and Jamal stood and shook hands with the ladies.

"It was nice meeting you, Ebony. I hope you'll stick around after our last set. The DJ will be throwing on some old-school tunes, and I'd love to continue where we left off," Maurice said.

"Well, I didn't have a curfew the last time I checked, so I guess we can hang around a bit."

A cool smile spread across Maurice's lips. "OK, I'll see you after the performance."

Ebony returned the smile. "I'll be here."

Chapter Six
Fire amd Desire

Maurice and Jamal returned backstage and bumped into Greg. They came up with a good idea to impress the ladies. After talking it over, Greg walked out and approached the table where the women sat.

"Excuse me, ladies, but I have a seat reserved for you. Please follow me."

"And who are you?" Stacy twisted her lips and rolled her neck.

"I apologize. My name is Greg, and I'm the owner of this establishment. A few good friends of mine suggested that a special table be reserved for you special ladies."

Monica stood up first. "What y'all waiting on?"

The women accompanied Greg toward the stage. All eyes were on Ebony as she strutted up front. Just to the left of the front row of tables were two empty tables labeled Reserved. Both tables had bottles of champagne chilling in buckets of ice. Greg pulled out the chairs at one of the tables for the women. They could view the band up close and were ecstatic.

"Enjoy the show." Greg smiled and proceeded backstage. The house lights dimmed and the soft jazz faded. Moments later, Greg walked out from behind the red curtain and grabbed the microphone.

"Ladies and gentlemen, I would like to thank you for coming out tonight. We have a special treat in store for you. Fellas, you'd better hold on to your ladies. Give a warm J'ville welcome to my good friend Brian McKnight!"

You could hear the crowd collectively gasp and then explode into applause when Brian McKnight stepped onto the stage. He waved at the crowd and blew kisses to the women in the audience. Everyone was stunned by the unexpected visit from the maestro himself.

The audience continued to applaud as the celebrity made his way to the reserved table next to Ebony, Monica, and Stacy. They were speechless and couldn't believe that they were actually sitting within arm's reach of Brian McKnight.

"Girl, I told you this was gonna be a good night!" Monica squealed with delight.

The applause subsided, and Greg continued. "Without further ado, ladies and gentlemen, I would like to introduce to you once again Jacksonville's own MoJazz!"

The curtains opened, and the club exploded once again. Maurice sat on a stool with the spotlight focused on him. The rest of the stage was dimly lit and decorated like an alley. Looking like an original ganster, Maurice wore a pinstriped suit and a matching pair of Stacy Adams.

Maurice kept his eyes on Ebony. He smiled and gave her a wink. Her perfect smile nearly melted his heart. He was thrilled by the look she had in her eyes.

Maurice pierced the silence as he blew into the soprano sax. He went into a solo and poured his heart into the piece, his hands softly caressing the instrument. Ebony couldn't help but get emotional. She felt every note he played as if it was meant for only her, and it was.

Maurice stood from the stool and proceeded down the stairs at the side of the stage, all the while staying perfectly on key and keeping his eyes on Ebony. The sax glistened in the spotlight as Maurice made his way down to Ebony's table.

He stood next to Ebony and got down on one knee and began to serenade her. She was so consumed in the moment that she didn't have time to feel embarrassed. There was a connection between them that they both felt. Her eyes began to water as he played the final note, and the crowded club clapped wildly.

Maurice grabbed her hand and gave it a soft kiss before taking a bow. He made his way back onto the stage, and Jamal came in on cue with a note that would've made even Johnny Gill sound like Milli Vanilli. After performing some vocal gymnastics, he began to talk to the crowd.

"Ladies, if you like what you see hold up your glass and save a drink for me. I will come by your table so we can meet. I'm Jamal, and this is MoJazz."

He deftly segued into the single that would hit the airwaves soon. "I want to know if Encounters is ready to 'Feel the Heat.'"

Women leaped to their feet, and the crowd went wild. Jamal went into a choral hoop that sounded like a Pentecostal preacher storming the pulpit at a T.D. Jakes convention.

"Baby, can you feel the heat?" he sang.

A lady in the front stood and shouted, "I'm on fire! Please come put this heat out!"

After Jamal did his job of getting the ladies moist, the band picked up the pace. Most of the room stood to their feet clapping and dancing. Chauncey plucked the bass like a black man with a piece of chicken on a deserted island. Devin's fingers smoothly glided across the ivory keys. Michael had the drums singing to the tunes of our forefathers as he tore up the percussion. The band mesmerized the audience for the next 45 minutes as they brought the house down.

The band finished their final set and received a standing ovation from the capacity crowd. Maurice introduced each band member and thanked everyone for coming out.

"Thanks for the love, J'ville! Don't forget to buy our single, 'Feel the Heat.' It'll hit the streets this summer. We hope you enjoyed us as much as we enjoyed you!"

One last bow, and the curtains closed.

Jamal jumped around backstage, still charged from the performance. "That was the shit, y'all!" he yelled.

Both Jamal and Maurice were anxious to pick up where they had left off with the ladies. They quickly packed up their equipment and had their usual after-show meeting in the dressing room. After 10 minutes, Maurice and Jamal fought their way past the usual gang of groupies hanging out backstage and headed out front to where Ebony and her friends were seated.

Ebony stood, gave Maurice a tight hug, and thanked him for making her feel so special. She was still ecstatic from meeting Brian McKnight. She pulled her camera out of her purse.

"I got some really good photos of Brian. I can't wait to develop these," she smiled broadly.

"Hope you enjoyed the show."

"The show was all that and a bag of chips!" Ebony replied.

The DJ took the joint to the next level when he threw on some old-school joints. The Peavey speakers boomed "Before I Let Go" by Frankie Beverly and Maze. A lot of couples headed for the dance floor near the stage.

Stacy grabbed Jamal's hand. "Oh, this is my song! Let's go dance."

"All right, Ms. Thang. Let's see what ya got." Jamal led her onto the dance floor.

"Would you like to dance, madam?" Maurice asked in a fake British accent.

"Why certainly, sir," Ebony replied in kind. They both shared a chuckle.

Ebony stood, and Maurice took a good look at her. Her dress firmly outlined her incredible figure. Her hips were curved in such a perfect formation that it would've made the designer of the Coke bottle sick with envy.

Maurice could feel his heart rate increase and his palms perspire. This woman had an inexplicable effect on him. He took her by the hand, and they strutted onto the dance floor.

They found a spot next to Jamal and Stacy, who were already getting their groove on.

"OK, girl! Shake that ass and show me what you working wit'!" Jamal demanded.

"Oh, you think you can handle this?" Stacy challenged. She turned her backside to Jamal and began to shake what her mama gave her. Her hips rotated and undulated to the beat.

Jamal had to almost pick his jaw up from the floor. Stacy was more than just a good dancer. She was a little too good, which made him wonder. He looked her up and down and paid attention to the way she danced. She gave a new definition of dropping it like it's hot.

She has got to be a stripper, he thought.

The way she moved was far too seductive and fluid. There was only one way to learn the type of moves she was throwing-- by practicing with a pole.

Monica made her way next to both couples as she danced with a young man sporting braids.

Aw shucks! Big girls need lovin', too, Jamal thought.

"Don't hurt 'em, Monica!" Stacy yelled.

"These whippersnappers can't handle all of this," Monica replied, shaking her rotund backside into the guy's crotch.

Stacy and Ebony both laughed as Monica manhandled the young buck.

After a few upbeat jams, the DJ slowed the pace and mixed in "Always and Forever." Couples just seemed to melt into each other's arms as if the scene were choreographed. Maurice and Ebony stared at each other for a short moment then followed suit. She didn't want to get too close, so she put her hands on his shoulder and they began to slow dance.

"You can get closer. I promise I won't bite," Maurice joked.

"I think this is close enough."

"What are you afraid of? You might like it."

"Don't flatter yourself, Horn Boy."

"I think you're just scared." Maurice winked.

"All right, Casanova. Just don't be feeling on my booty, or I'll have to check you right here on the dance floor." Ebony latched her arms around his neck. His massive hands squeezed around her petite waist and they continued to slow drag. She felt comfortable and relaxed in Maurice's arms.

His eyes dug deep into her as they danced silently. He admired the beautiful contours of her lovely face: her high cheekbones, lusciously full lips, and deep dimples when she smiled. One thing was for sure; no other woman made him feel what he was feeling at that moment. Ebony laid her head on his chest, and they lost themselves for the next four minutes.

After the song was over, Ebony and Maurice headed back to the table. Jamal and Stacy were still grinding it on the dance floor for the next few songs. Monica and her newfound friend were getting closer than close as well.

"So are you enjoying yourself, Ebony?" Maurice asked.

"I'm having a good time. How about you?"

"Let's just say I haven't had this much fun in a long time."

Ebony rolled her eyes like only she could do. "Come on now. I'm sure you've had better times."

"I'm serious. I really enjoy your company."

Ebony blushed a bit as she nodded her head. *I'm enjoying your company too*, she thought.

"So what is it you do for a living?" Maurice inquired.

"I'm a photographer."

"Oh, I see that you're a creative soul as well."

"I try my best." She took another sip of her drink.

"So are you originally from Jacksonville?" Maurice asked.

"No, actually I'm from Louisiana. I moved here about a year ago. I like it so far."

"What part of Louisiana are you from?"

"I'm from Lafayette, which is 40 minutes from Baton Rouge."

"I know the place. I have some family back in New Iberia, so I've passed through Lafayette before. So that explains your exotic look. You have a little Creole in the family."

"Yeah, I'm from a Creole bloodline."

"I'm sure you can throw down in the kitchen." He winked.

Ebony smiled, her dimples sinking deep into her cheeks. "I can do a little somethin' somethin'."

"I bet you can," Maurice flirted.

The others returned from the dance floor and took their seats. Monica came back fanning herself with her hand, beads of sweat rolling down her face. Her young conquest followed behind.

"Everyone, this is Hakeem," she said.

They all shook hands.

"Hey, yo, that set y'all did was off the chain! Y'all got mad skills!" said Hakeem.

Maurice and Jamal dapped him up.

"Thanks, bro. Just make sure you peep our single when it's released," Maurice replied.

"No doubt," Hakeem said.

They all sat around and conversed about a multitude of subjects. As the evening progressed, everyone showed signs of fatigue.

Jamal yawned loudly and stretched. "Ladies, it seems to be getting pretty late. I think it's time I retire. Stacy, would you allow me to give you a ride back home?"

I thought you'd never ask, Stacy thought. "Sure, Jamal, I'm down with that. Girlfriends, I'll see you later." Stacy stood and winked at Monica.

"It was nice meeting you, Ebony, Monica." Jamal dapped Maurice.

"It was nice meeting you as well. You guys have a good night. Call me in the morning, Stacy," Monica said.

Jamal knew what that meant. Monica wanted blow-by-blow details, and he figured he'd give her friend something to talk about.

"Yeah, you guys take care," said Ebony.

Monica and Hakeem were also getting ready to make a break for the exit. There was no shame in her game as she made it known that she was going to tear into this young stud and show him what a big girl was working with.

"Ebony, I'm going to get outta here and into something else." She nodded toward Hakeem.

Ebony looked at her cousin like her head was beginning to shrink. "So how am I supposed to get home?" Ebony asked.

Maurice eagerly butted into the conversation. "I'll be more than happy to take you home. Trust me, I'm not some deranged psycho."

Ebony gave Monica the "I'm going to kill you for this" look as Maurice sat smiling.

69

"Fine then. I guess Maurice will take me home. I'll deal with you later." Ebony scowled at her cousin.

"Take care of my girl, Mr. MoJazz."

"Don't worry, Monica. She's in good hands."

Maurice and Ebony stood and headed for the door. They walked hand in hand through the crowd. Ebony held onto his arm, and Maurice could feel tingles up and down his spine at her touch. Just being close to her turned him on.

Ebony felt the same way as she held tightly onto his arm. Walking out of the club, it was as if all eyes were on them.

"What a beautiful couple," a woman standing near the exit commented.

Ebony was definitely enjoying the attention she got from being with Mr. Tall, Dark, and Handsome, but she did a good job of hiding it.

Chapter Seven
Watch Out Now

Jamal and Stacy walked hand in hand to his truck, which was parked around the corner of the building near the back entrance. The rear parking lot was filled with people loitering. Both men and women were running game and making last-ditch efforts to score. Big D was in the parking lot barking orders, trying his best to disperse the crowd.

"Y'all don't have to go home, but you got to get the hell outta here!" he yelled.

Reluctantly people began to start moving toward their cars. Stacy held onto Jamal's arm like she didn't want to let go while they walked and talked. Both she and Jamal knew they were in for a long night of boot-knocking.

As they approached Jamal's Navigator, both of them noticed a piece of paper lying under his windshield wiper blade.

"Damn solicitors," Jamal grunted as he picked up the paper. Just before he was about to ball it up, he turned it over and read it.

YOU'LL GET WHAT'S COMING TO YOU, JAMAL!
I'M WATCHING YOU!

What the hell is this? he thought.

Jamal's expression quickly turned grim. He glanced around the parking lot, searching for a hint as to who might have left the note. He cursed under his breath and wadded up the paper, throwing it on the ground.

"Are you all right?" Concern filled Stacy's voice.

"Yeah, I'm aw'ight. Damn salespeople are always leaving junk on your car." He played it off as smoothly as he could.

"That's the truth," Stacy agreed. "And I can't stand those damn telemarketers either. Every time you turn around, there's another one trying to sell you something. Hell, they even have a recorded voice that calls your home now."

Jamal opened the door for Stacy, and she climbed into the truck. She was going on and on about telemarketers while Jamal shut the passenger door. He was pissed off. He didn't know who'd left the note for him, but he intended to find out. On the way out of the parking lot, he stopped by the entrance and yelled for Big D.

"Hey, Big D. Come here for a minute."

The gargantuan bouncer walked over to the truck, looking like he just finished hurting someone.

"Did you notice anything suspicious tonight?" Jamal asked.

"Man, this place has been so packed that I can't say that I would've recognized anything out of the ordinary. Why, what's up?" Big D asked.

"It's nothing, but do me a favor and keep a close eye on the ride when we come back Tuesday night."

"Not a problem, J. Maurice already told me that you guys may be hirin' for road security and he'd like me to be a bodyguard."

"That's cool, big dog. Just keep an eye out for me." They dapped each other.

"No doubt, bro. I'll be on the lookout. I'll holla."

"Peace out, big man." Jamal rolled up his window and drove away.

Chapter Eight
Get To Know Ya

Maurice and Ebony sat quietly in the car as he shifted the roadster into fifth gear and merged onto I-95 South. They both bobbed their heads to Maxwell singing about how fortunate he was to have this woman in his life. Maurice hoped he'd be singing the same tune if Ebony turned out to be as sweet as she appeared.

He turned the volume down because he was more interested in talking with Ebony. He wanted to get to know this beautiful brown goddess. A creature of habit, Maurice found his eyes constantly straying toward her legs. Her dress climbed up her thighs when she moved in the seat, revealing her sexy legs.

Ebony's legs were muscularly toned and contoured to near- perfection. The open-toe heels she wore displayed her French- manicured toes. Even her toes were appealing, which was a thought that Maurice relished since he had a foot fetish. Ebony sat with her arms crossed, trying her best to relax. She could feel his eyes crawling all over her. When she felt that Maurice was looking, she quickly turned and busted him.

"Is there a problem?" she asked playfully.

"No, not at all. I was just wondering if you were an aerobics instructor or something. You have really nice legs," Maurice coyly replied, knowing he was cold busted.

Ebony smiled at his demeanor. He had player written all over his face, but she just couldn't resist his boyish charm.

"I do a little TaeBo every now and then."

"With legs like that, you should be on someone's swimsuit calendar."

"Flattery will get you everywhere." Ebony blushed and tried in vain to pull her dress further down her leg. "I guess all those years of running track paid off."

"Where'd you go to school?"

"I attended Southern University. I ran track there for a few years."

"The Jaguars. Yeah, I remember we used to battle y'all during football halftime shows."

"You were in a marching band?"

"The Florida A&M Marching One Hundred, baby!" Maurice boasted. "I remember when we played you guys at the Circle City Classic in Indianapolis."

"Oh yeah, and what happened?"

"The Rattlers had to represent and show y'all how we do it in Florida. We also won the football game."

"Well, that's no surprise. We never had a good football team. What they need is a good female coach."

Maurice looked over at Ebony. "Now what do *you* know about football?" he asked sarcastically.

"A lot more than you think," she shot back.

"Really?"

"Try me."

"Well, Ms. Thang, tell me who's the all-time leading rusher in the NFL."

Ebony turned and faced Maurice with her arms folded. "Aw come on, you have to come better than that." Ebony laughed. "Everyone knows that Walter Payton holds the record."

Maurice laughed. "So it's like that," Maurice replied. "Then tell me who has the most rushing touchdowns in Super Bowl history?

Ebony put her hand on her chin and thought for a moment. "That would be Emmitt Smith when he rushed for five touchdowns."

Maurice was so surprised that he nearly choked on the Big Red gum he was chewing.

"Are you OK?" Ebony patted him on the back.

Maurice rolled down the window and spit out the gum. "I must say I'm impressed, Ms. Stanford," Maurice said after he regained his composure. "You're the first woman I've met who really knows football."

Ebony smiled. "Told you I had skills."

"I stand corrected." Maurice conceded.

"I've always been a sports fanatic. I still do a lot of running. Gotta stay in shape for the River Run."

"I've been known to tear up the asphalt every now and then. I was thinking about getting in shape for the River Run myself." Maurice said, knowing good and well he wasn't a distance runner.

"Oh really? You can run with me whenever your schedule permits."

"All righty then, Jackie Joyner-Kersee. Whenever you're ready."

"My girlfriend and I train at the Sandalwood High track on Sundays. If you're up for it, we'll be there in the morning." Ebony wondered if Maurice would seize the opportunity to get together so soon. She didn't want to seem desperate, but she wanted to see Maurice again--soon.

"You ain't said nothing but a thang! I'll meet you there. What time?" Maurice asked.

"About ten o'clock."

"Damn, guess I better try to get some sleep."

"That might be a good idea, Horn Boy. If you want to try to run with this female, you'll need all the rest you can get. By the way, I'll have an ambulance waiting in the parking lot when you pass out." Ebony laughed.

She's joking, but I might need one since I haven't run in a long time, he thought.

Ebony admired Maurice's luscious lips. She wanted to reach over and softly bite them. Her mind drifted into a fantasy. She pictured him using those adorable lips to kiss her entire body. She snapped back to reality after a minute and tried to dismiss the thought. It'd been a very long time since she let a man touch her, but her body longed for it.

She reached in her purse and pulled out another stick of Big Red. "Here's a piece to replace the one you nearly choked on."

"Thanks. I hope my breath hasn't started kicking."

"Like Billy Blanks."

"Thanks for the candid analogy." They both cracked up.

Ebony unwrapped the stick of gum, reached over, and put it in his mouth. She softly grazed his lips with her fingertip and said, "You have nice lips."

"Thanks."

He'd become accustomed to compliments about them. Everyone in high school used to tease him about having big lips. But in this day and age, most women found them very attractive and he made sure to put them to good use.

"So how did you get into photography?" he asked.

Ebony's face lit up when he mentioned her favorite conversation piece. "I've always enjoyed pictures ever since I was a kid. I'd walk around the neighborhood and just sit and look at the way certain places seemed to talk to me."

"I'd like to take a look at your work some time. I know a little about shooting frames myself."

"I guess you're just quite the Renaissance man, huh?" She smirked.

"Something like that. I'm also a psychic."

"Oh really? So tell me what I'm thinking, Mr. Cleo."

"Right now you're thinking, 'Oh my God, this is the finest brotha I've ever seen! He's just so sweet!'" Maurice joked.

Ebony burst out in a fit of laughter. "Well, I guess you better keep your day job as a musician 'cause someone would see that you're a fraud as a psychic."

"A brotha can't get no love," he laughed. "So tell me what brought you out here to Jacksonville?" Maurice changed the subject.

Ebony turned and stared out the passenger window. She didn't want to remember or recount anything about her reasons for moving away from Louisiana. A few silent moments passed without an answer.

"Is everything all right?" Maurice inquired.

"It's a long story that I'd rather not talk about."

"In case you ever want to talk, just let me know. I'm also a shrink by day."

Ebony turned and smiled. "Well, every now and then I could use a shrink. You know a sistah's got issues to resolve."

"Who doesn't have issues? The world is a crazy place these days. Nothing like when we were growing up."

"Ain't that the truth." Ebony agreed. "So how did you get into music?" Ebony asked.

"It's always been my passion. I come from a long line of musicians. My mother taught me how to play the piano when I was young. I guess I just never looked back."

"Is your mother here in Jacksonville?"

"No, she passed away about four years ago," Maurice replied.

"Oh my, I'm so sorry."

"That's OK; you didn't know. She was really a remarkable woman. I just wish she was still here."

"How about your father?" Ebony inquired. She knew she must've hit a sour note due to the acerbic expression on Maurice's face.

"I don't know where my father is and don't give a damn. He and my mom divorced when I was younger. We left Birmingham and ended up here in Jacksonville. I haven't seen the man since."

"I know what it's like growing up without parents. I lost both of my parents in a car accident when I was 10 years old," Ebony frowned.

"Damn, that must've been tough to deal with."

"No doubt. I lived with my grandmother until I enrolled in college. I've always been driven in everything I put my hand to. I feel like they're looking down at me, and I don't want to disappoint them. That keeps me going," Ebony said.

"That's a point of motivation. I'm kinda the same way with music. I picture my mother sitting in the front row with a huge smile as she hears me play. But tonight I had a different inspiration." Maurice could see Ebony smiling in his peripheral vision.

"Well, I'd like to hear you play again," Ebony said.

"If you like, I'll give you a private performance. Like the song says--just you and I."

Ebony blushed. "All right, Casanova, don't start nothing you can't finish."

"I'm always a good finisher." Maurice smiled.

They'd just exited off I-95 and turned onto Bay Meadows Road. Maurice downshifted the roadster as they approached the light.

"Make a left at the light. I'm over at Hollow Pines on the right," Ebony directed. They pulled into the parking lot of her apartment complex shortly thereafter.

"Thanks for bringing me home, Maurice."

"The pleasure was all mine."

Maurice got out of the car and ran to the other side to open the door for her. Ebony stepped out of the passenger side, and he noticed those nicely shaped legs and her calf muscles flex when she stood.

"I'll walk you to the door."

"Sure, that's fine," Ebony replied.

She was hoping that Maurice wouldn't ask to be invited in. The way she was feeling at the moment she knew it wouldn't take much before both of them would be wrestling between her sheets. She knew that shouldn't happen--at least not yet.

Maurice took her by the hand and led her down the walkway leading to her apartment.

"Thanks for the wonderful evening. I've enjoyed your company, and I'm looking forward to seeing you tomorrow," Maurice said.

She knew he'd probably said the same thing to more than a hundred women, but for some reason she believed his sincerity. "Same here, Maurice. I'm looking forward to tomorrow as well."

"Should I pick you up?"

"No, I have to stop by the photo studio in the morning, so I'll just meet you at the track around ten. You know where Sandalwood High School is, right?"

"Yeah, I know where it is."

A few moments of silence passed as their eyes locked. He kissed her on the forehead and said goodnight.

Finally a gentleman, she thought. She assumed that he would try to make a move on her and get inside, but he never once tried to go there.

Maurice walked back down the breezeway to his car, feeling like he'd just hit the lottery. Ebony stood holding the keys in the door and watching him as he walked away. She wanted to invite him in but figured it would be better not to rush into things. She wondered if he would give her one last look.

Maurice walked away with a bounce in his step. Before turning the corner to step out of view, he paused and turned to look over his shoulder. Sure enough, Ebony was still standing at the door watching him. They both smiled and   waved   goodnight.

When he got back to the car, he cheered, "Yeeeeees!"

This night turned out to be just what he was looking for. He finally met someone who aroused all his senses, both physically and mentally. He sped off with delight, bumping to the tunes of Musiq. Simon was right.

Chapter Nine
Girl Talk

Ebony was glad she listened to Monica and joined them for a night on the town. It turned out to be one of the most memorable nights she'd had in years. She didn't want to get her expectations up; after all, she'd just met the man. But Ebony remembered the passion and sincerity in his eyes when he played that song for her. Even though it was too soon to tell, Ebony discerned that there was something about Maurice LaSalle that said *forever*.

After taking a brief shower, Ebony slipped into her favorite teddy from Victoria's Secret. She then picked up her Eric Jerome Dickey novel *Cheaters*. Her personal library was filled with his novels as well as works from Michael Baisden, Marcus Major, and Travis Hunter. She immersed herself into the world of fiction every night before she went to bed. Novels provided a place to retreat and release the stress that had accumulated during the day.

After reading a few lines, she found it hard to focus. All she could think about was Maurice. She sat the book on the nightstand and lay in bed staring at the ceiling.

The sensual ache between her legs was beginning to peak. She grabbed a pillow and placed it between them, squeezing it tight.

"Damn, I should've invited him up," she mumbled.

She pictured herself onstage with Maurice, just the two of them, dancing slowly as the spotlight kissed the top of their heads. Maurice's hands softly caressed her, the same way he skillfully caressed his instrument. The moment made her think of the "Spanish Guitar" video by Toni Braxton. She could relate to what Toni was saying in that song.

Just as Ebony reached over to turn off the lamp, she noticed the message light blinking on her answering machine. She pressed the answer button to retrieve her messages.

You have two new messages.

First message at 6:32 p.m.: Ebony, baby, this is your Aunt Shirley. Would you tell your good-for-nothing cousin to give me a call? She acts like she can't call her mama anymore! Talk to you later, sweetie.

Next message at 11:45 p.m.: Hey, girl, this is Charlene. Just wanted to let you know that I'm back in town. Where are you this time of night? Anyway, give me a shout when you get back in.

Charlene was Ebony's best friend since she'd moved to Jacksonville. They both shared a keen interest in photography and sports. Charlene had been in Tampa for the past week visiting her sister. Ebony was anxious to tell her what happened at the club. She glanced over at the clock hanging above her vanity. It was 2:15 a.m.

Charlene's probably asleep, but I'll wake her up anyway, she thought.

She picked up the phone and dialed Charlene's number. After the third ring, a sleepy voice answered the phone.

"Hello?"

"Wake up, girl. I can't believe you're asleep this early," Ebony said.

"What's up, girlfriend? Shit, why are you calling me this late at night sounding all happy?" Charlene groggily asked.

"I just had to tell you what went down tonight. I went out with Monica and Stacy. We had a good time down at Encounters."

"What? You mean to tell me you actually went out for a change."

"Yes, ma'am, and I'm glad I did. I hadn't enjoyed myself like that in a long time, not to mention that I ended up meeting this fine-ass brotha named Maurice," Ebony spoke with girlish excitement. "He just dropped me off."

"Just dropped you off?" Charlene asked. "If he was that fine, why didn't you go home with him?"

"Nah, girl, I'm not like the rest of you hoes."

"Nothing's wrong with being a little ho-ish every now and then. So what happened?" Charlene sounded awake all of a sudden.

"He just dropped me off and we said goodnight, that's all."

"Girl, I know you didn't wake me up just to tell me a guy dropped you off. I could see if you wanted to tell me that he *broke* you off."

"It was tempting, but I didn't wanna go to that level on the first night. Hell, this wasn't even an official date. The only reason he gave me a ride is because Monica and Stacy wanted to go get their freak on."

Charlene shook her head. "I can't believe you met a guy at a club. You're the one always talking about how all the guys in clubs aren't worth a damn."

"I know, I know. You're preaching to the choir. But there's just something about this man--something more than just his good looks."

"So what does this man do?" Charlene inquired.

Ebony knew that question was coming. Charlene was always giving lectures about dating a man who's gainfully employed with good credit.

"He's a musician with the band that plays in the jazz club," Ebony replied.

"A musician? You see, now you're asking for trouble. You know what type of life those guys live!"

"Well, check this out. While he was playing, we made eye contact for a quick moment. Then he took a second look in the middle of his solo. At first I wasn't sure if he was looking at me. So I smiled, and he winked back."

"Aw, now doesn't that sound so sweet," Charlene said sarcastically.

Ebony rolled her eyes. "Well, after their set, he came over to the table and introduced himself. We talked for a moment, and the vibe was real strong. Then once they went backstage to start the second set, the club owner came to our table. Next thing you know he's leading us to a reserved table in front of the stage!"

"Do I really have to hear all this?"

"Well, here's the good part. Before the band went back on, they introduced a celebrity who made a cameo appearance!"

"Really?" Charlene sat up in bed.

"Girl, you're going to die when I tell you who came onto the stage."

"Who, girl, who?" Charlene pleaded.

"Brian McKnight!"

"You're shitting me! Are you serious?" Charlene screamed. She was a huge Brian McKnight fan. She couldn't believe she'd missed the opportunity of a lifetime to finally meet him.

"That's not the best part. He sat at the table right next to us."

"I knew I didn't want to hear this! So did you get the chance to talk to him?"

"Yeah, we all got autographs. He's even finer in person."

Charlene sighed, "Damn, I knew I should've come back earlier."

"Once the band started playing again, Maurice walked off the stage while playing his solo. He came up to our table and serenaded me with his saxophone."

"Aren't you just Ms. Lucky."

"Girl, I'm glad I finally went out."

"Well, I'm glad to hear you finally had some fun. Lord knows you deserve it. Anyway, I'll be hitting the track at the usual time. You with me, right?" Charlene asked.

"I'll be ready. Oh, and by the way, I invited Maurice to join us."

"You did? Damn, I guess you are serious. I definitely have to meet this brotha."

"He'll meet us at the track at ten o'clock," Ebony said.

"This brotha better be fine as hell to have you calling me this early in morning just to give me the 411."

"He's got it going on; you'll see. Well, I'm out, I'll see you later in the morning."

"All right then. I'll meet you at the track. I gotta get some more sleep."

"I will too--after I play with Bam Bam," Ebony laughed.

"Bye, horny heifer."

"Bye, girl," Ebony replied.

After her vibrating companion helped to cool off her burning pleasure center, Ebony closed her eyes so she could get some sleep. The image of Maurice kept tugging at her mind and all she could think about was the man and his saxophone. She wondered what he was doing at that very same moment.

Chapter Ten
Run To You

It was 9:45 a.m. when Ebony and Charlene arrived at Sandalwood High School's athletic track. It was cool and breezy, which made it a perfect morning for running. The annual 5K River Run was only a month away, and both women were looking forward to participating in the race. The track was already a bit overcrowded due to the spring flingers trying their best to get in shape before the summer months rolled around.

An elderly African-American couple walked briskly around the track holding hands, both dressed in matching Reebok outfits. The look on their faces told a story of love and happiness.

Ebony observed their happiness. *What an Al Green moment*, she thought. She wondered if it was still possible to have such a special union in this day and age. Or if it was just a fantasy that young women dreamed about when they were little girls.

Charlene looked around, anxiously waiting to meet this Maurice guy who Ebony had been talking about all night and morning. She knew he had to be something special because many a man had tried to date Ebony, but most were just left hung out to dry with bruised egos.

"So where's this sexy musician of yours?" Charlene asked.

"I'm sure he'll be here. It's not even ten o'clock yet."

"I can't believe you. I go out of town for a few days and, when I get back, my best friend has fallen all in love."

Ebony smirked. "I'm not in love with the man, Charlene. There's just something about him that I'm feeling."

"You sure that's not your hormones you're feeling? You know you haven't had any dick in a long time."

"Now don't you start. I hear enough of that from my cousin and her slutty friend," Ebony retorted.

"Well, it's the truth. I was beginning to think you had some kind of freaky thing going on with that camera of yours. Either that or you were going lesbian on me."

Ebony laughed, "Girl, please, I'm all woman. There's nothing like a good stiff one--for sure."

Charlene looked her friend up and down. "Just checking."

"I'm not trying to take a vow of celibacy or anything like that. I'm waiting for the right time."

"I can't hate on you for wanting to do it like that," Charlene chided.

Ebony put her hands on her hips. "I'm sure Maurice will get a chance to taste these cookies--as long as he acts right."

"Just be careful, girlfriend. You know how these fools are around here. Always playing these head games just so they can get the panties and split."

"I hear ya, but I really think there's something different about Maurice. He seems to be a man of substance."

"Uh huh. I can see it in your eyes already."

Ebony looked shocked at Charlene's statement. "See what?"

"Come on, girl, don't try to deny it!"

Charlene began singing the old hit song by the Rude Boys, "Written All Over Your Face."

Ebony playfully punched Charlene in the arm. "Well, what can I say? I know we just met last night, but the connection was indescribable. He's one romantic motherfucker!"

Charlene just shook her head. "Yeah, that's how it usually starts off. Then after they've gotten into your panties it's like, 'Who are you?'"

"At least try to be a little optimistic. Give a sistah a break."

"Aw'ight then. I'm just saying be careful."

"I won't rush into anything. We'll just take it slow," Ebony responded.

Charlene's attention was diverted as she stared over Ebony's shoulder. Ebony turned around to see what had distracted her.

On the other side of the track was a well-toned man beginning his warm-up run. The man strode like he was training for the Olympic team. He was wearing black spandex shorts and a muscle shirt that hugged his torso. His muscular striations were visible from a far distance. He increased his speed to an all out sprint as he made his way into the third quarter leg of the track. Both women felt googly eyed as the African Adonis made his way toward them.

"You see that fine-ass man over there running? Damn, now that's what I call a Mandingo!" Charlene licked her lips at the sight.

"Yeah, he is fine." Ebony conceded.

The man turned the last curve on the track, looking better than Michael Johnson as he reduced his stride and slowed. He turned from the track and then began slowly trotting to the center field where Ebony and Charlene were stretching. Once he'd gotten close enough to be recognized, Ebony's eyes lit up like a spotlight piercing the night. Maurice ran right up to Ebony and picked her up by the waist. He spun her around a few times, and she playfully screamed, "Put me down! Put me down!"

Maurice put her down and gave her a kiss on the cheek. "Sorry I'm running late. I'm never on time. I'll probably be late for my own funeral."

Charlene cleared her throat.

"Maurice, I'd like you to meet my girl Charlene." Ebony stepped aside to introduce them.

Maurice noticed how fine Charlene was. Her figure was just as attractive as Ebony's. *Birds of feather flock together*, he thought.

Charlene was wearing high-cut biker shorts that revealed a whole lot of junk in her trunk. The Reebok sports bra made her breasts look inviting. She made a brotha wanna say "Aww" like Cameo's Larry Blackmon. Maurice reached out to shake her hand. He stuttered and caught himself before he called her Candy, after Cameo's jam.

"Nice to meet you, Charlene."

"It's nice to meet you too." Charlene held onto his hand a little longer than necessary.

"All right now, that's enough," Ebony joked.

"Damn, Ebony, you weren't lying. He sure is fine."

Maurice grinned. "I see somebody's been talking about me."

The ladies chuckled.

"Are you already warmed up?" Ebony asked.

"Yeah, I stretched out in the parking lot and got a quick sprint around the track," he replied.

"You sure you can keep up?" she teased.

"Woman, how do you think I got these powerful lungs to blow into that sax?" Maurice was an avid gym buff, but he wasn't into running long distances. Just getting warmed up nearly had him sucking wind.

"Well, this ain't any musical performance, Kenny G. You sure you can hang?" Charlene joked.

"Y'all ain't said anything but a thang. Let's do like Marvin Gaye and get it on!" Maurice replied.

All three of them stepped onto the track and got in a last-minute stretch. Maurice noticed he and Ebony had the same type of MP3 player strapped on their waists.

"I guess we do have a lot in common." Maurice pointed to her MP3 player.

Ebony smiled and started the timer on her watch. She then looked over at Charlene. "Charlene, you want to set the pace?"

"OK, I'll pace, but y'all better keep up."

"I know you're talking to Horn Boy back there. Let's see how much he can really blow," Ebony said as they began a slow jog.

"Don't worry about me. I know I can hang. The question is can y'all hang with me?" Maurice boasted.

"Pa-lease!" Charlene squealed. "Just remember that second place is first losers!"

Charlene always loved a challenge. She was a very competitive person and didn't want to settle for second place. Maurice remained a few paces behind Ebony as they trotted in a single-file line. He enjoyed the view of watching the fluid motion of her booty. The rise and fall of the muscles in her legs let Maurice know that he wasn't running with an amateur.

Charlene was out front striding and setting the pace for the 12 laps around the asphalt. Charlene's legs were muscularly toned, and she had just as much if not more booty genes as Ebony. After the first lap, Maurice ran alongside Ebony instead of pacing behind her.

"So how many of these marathons have you run in?" he asked between huffs and puffs.

"This will be my second one here in Jacksonville. I'm not a veteran like Charlene."

"How about you, Charlene?"

"This'll be my seventh," Charlene yelled, with a tinge of pride in her voice.

Maurice had never participated in a marathon. He was more of a sprinter than a distance runner. Though he'd run track during his high school years, he could tell that old age had gotten the best of him.

"You might want to save that wind of yours, Mr. Sax Man. We've got a lot of laps to run," Ebony teased.

"I told you, I've got a good set of lungs."

"We'll see if you'll be singing the same tune after a few more laps," Ebony countered.

She turned up the volume on her MP3 player to help her get into a rhythm. She effortlessly bounced around the track. Maurice could feel his legs starting to burn. They'd just passed the mile marker at five minutes and fifty seconds. Charlene had set the pace a little fast.

Damn, eight more laps to go, he thought.

Maurice regretted stopping by McDonald's and eating that sausage Egg McMuffin for breakfast. Every step he took re-enforced the fact that he'd made a bad choice. He increased the volume on his Nomad player so he could take his mind off the pain churning under the left side of his rib cage.

The beats of the Ruff Ryders thumped through his earphones as he listened to DMX talk about losing his mind up in here. The rhythmic Swizz Beatz tracks helped keep Maurice's mind off the pain, but only for a few minutes. That's when his legs began to feel like Swiss cheese.

Ebony and Charlene looked like professional runners as they increased their stride with smooth kicks. Their jaws were hanging loosely from their faces, their arms swinging back and forth in a relaxed motion.

Maurice found it difficult to keep up with the two gazelles. They were both striding gracefully like they were in their natural habitat. He fell about 10 yards behind the women and began to suck wind. His legs burned ferociously. The mental battle of running long distances was getting the best of him.

Ebony couldn't feel his presence behind her. She looked over her shoulder and noticed he'd fallen a few yards back. She smiled and gave him a wink.

"Looks like the Horn Boy can't keep up," she joked.

Charlene looked back and laughed. Maurice knew he was about to become the object of ridicule. The taste of McMuffin lay stagnant in his throat. He struggled to keep his breathing in short rhythmic beats. His lungs were now burning like a $3 crack whore.

How in the hell did I get myself into this? he thought.

Chasing after the opposite sex made many a man do some really strange things. Maurice had never trained for a marathon. He willed his body to keep going, but that sharp pain on his left side was becoming unbearable.

After the two-mile point, Maurice had given up all hope of catching Marion Jones and Flo Jo. He'd fallen too far behind and his lungs burned so badly that they felt as if he had just finished singing with Lucifer in Hades. Maurice trotted off of the track and collapsed onto the grass in center field.

What the hell was I thinking? he wondered.

Charlene and Ebony continued their kick around the track, moving in sync with each other. Maurice felt foolish as he lay down on the grass. He knew he wasn't going to hear the end of this one.

After the ladies finished their mini-marathon, they jogged over to center field. Maurice was still lying down with his eyes closed, listening to music.

Ebony gave him a slight kick on the shoulder. "What's up, Horn Boy? I thought you were all that on the track. You were talking all that trash, and you couldn't even finish the race."

"Looks like the man with the mighty lungs doesn't have any stamina," Charlene interjected.

I hope he has endurance in the bed, Ebony thought.

"Just give me a few weeks, and we'll see who rules the track. I shouldn't have eaten that McDonald's this morning."

"Excuses, excuses. Just admit that you got your butt whipped," Ebony said.

"I'm man enough to admit it. But payback is such sweet revenge. Like I said, just give me a few weeks."

"Whatever, Horn Boy."

Charlene turned to Ebony. "So what's on the agenda for today?" Charlene asked.

Maurice quickly spoke up. "Ebony, I would love you to be my guest at dinner tonight. That's if you're free, of course."

Ebony smiled and felt warm and tingly inside. "Charlene, it looks like I'm going to dinner tonight."

"That sounds romantic. Sure I can't tag along?" Charlene teased.

Ebony gave her an "Are you crazy" look. "Nah, Ms. Thang, it's just me and my man tonight! You got to get your own."

"I'm just joking," Charlene replied. She looked over at Maurice. "So are you going to join us on the track next week?"

Maurice shook his head, still holding his aching side. "I don't know if I'm up for this running thang. I think I better stick to what I do best."

Charlene laughed, "Aw come on, big timer. You were talking all that smack when we first got started."

"Yeah, I told you that you couldn't hang," Ebony joined in.

"I know, I know," Maurice conceded, knowing it would be a long time before he heard the end of this one.

"My girl tells me you're very good with the saxophone," Charlene said.

"That's an understatement. He can make that thing talk," Ebony replied.

"I do my thang. You ought to stop by and check out the show."

Charlene nodded her head. "Yeah, I think I'll do that."

Maurice's cell phone rang as they all walked to the parking lot. He looked at the caller ID and there wasn't a number listed. He answered the phone.

"Hello?"

"Hey, you," Carmen said.

Maurice turned away from Ebony and Charlene. "Hey, what's up?"

"Not much, I was just thinking about you and thought I'd give you a holler."

"How sweet of you," Maurice semi-whispered. He knew Ebony and Charlene were probably burning holes in his back with their eyes. He knew that all women have that insatiable sense of curiosity, especially if they feel another woman could be involved. He stepped away and tried to quickly wrap up the conversation.

Charlene looked at Ebony and nudged her head toward Maurice. "You see how he walked away when the phone rang? It must be his woman," she advised.

"Come on now, Charlene. How can you go jumping to that conclusion? It could be a business call, for all we know."

"A business call on a Sunday morning? Please tell me you're not that naïve."

"Don't even go there." Ebony sucked her teeth.

100

Maurice ended his conversation with Carmen and walked back to where the women stood. "I'd love to hang around, ladies, but I have to get going."

Charlene looked at Ebony out of the corner of her eye. "Uh huh," she said softly.

"OK, sweetie, I'll see you later tonight." Ebony gave him a kiss on the cheek.

"Be ready by seven," Maurice said.

"I'll be waiting," Ebony replied.

"It was nice meeting you, Charlene." Maurice extended his hand.

"Nice meeting you too." Charlene shook his hand, allowing it to linger again.

Maurice walked toward his car and hopped in.

Charlene turned to Ebony. "Well, he is as fine as you said, but he seems like a dog to me."

"Really? What makes you say that?"

"The way he walked away when his phone rang. He just strikes me as the type who likes to run game."

Ebony became agitated. She threw her hands up to the sky. "Could you at least be a little bit optimistic?"

Charlene folded her arms in a defensive posture. After a few awkward moments of silence, she smiled. "As long as you're happy, then I'm happy."

Ebony returned with a smile of her own.

Chapter Eleven

Atomic Dog

Jamal was in the kitchen drinking a Myoplex protein shake. He'd just completed his usual grueling workout regiment at the gym. He spent countless hours in the gym making sure that his physique was up to par. Just as he finished off the last of his shake, the phone rang. He walked over and picked it up from the counter.

"Hello?"

"What's up, pimp daddy?" Maurice said.

"Not much, bro. Just getting back from the gym."

"So how did things go with ol' girl last night?"

Jamal took a seat in his favorite recliner. "Man, I threw down my mack lines, and she was down for whatever.

We went over to her place, and it was on and poppin'! I don't think she'll be walking straight for about a week. What about you and her friend? I know you beat up the cookies."

"Nah, bro, I just gave her a ride back to her place, we hugged, and said goodnight."

"What?" Jamal griped, his voice an octave higher than usual. "You mean to tell me you didn't tear into that fine piece of chocolate?"

"She's not a Hershey bar and, no, I didn't tear into it."

Jamal pulled the phone away from his ear and gave it a look of astonishment. "Slow down, Casanova Brown. I haven't heard you catching feelings like this about a woman in a long time. Tell me you at least tongued her down and got those panties wet."

"Nah, man, we just hugged and said goodnight."

Jamal shook his head. "You're holding out on me, right?"

Maurice laughed. "I'm serious, man, I was really feeling her, and I didn't want to go out like that on the first night."

"Oh no! I don't believe this shit! Don't tell me you're sprung after the first night and you didn't even get to test drive the goods! Didn't I teach you anything?"

"I didn't know I was enrolled in Players University, Professor Grover."

"And you are about to get expelled, nigga! This is serious business, bro! You know how much ass is going to be coming our way once we finish this album?"

Maurice made an extra effort not to tell Jamal about meeting Ebony at the track that morning. Jamal would've just gone on and on about how not to sweat a woman so soon, especially when he didn't bust a nut.

"It's not like I'm going to marry the girl or something. I was just really feeling her. She got my attention, that's all."

Uh oh, I bet he's got that damn look in his eyes, Jamal thought. "Oh yeah, you're gone, man. That's the first step in that old saying: Touch my mind, you have my attention. Touch my heart, you have my love. Touch my soul, you have my will. Next thing you know you'll be hearing wedding bells and Keith Sweat will be crying in the background. Man, that shit's for the birds. Ain't no woman getting half of Jamal."

"Don't you think you're jumping the gun, bro? I don't plan on getting into that situation for a long time. I'm enjoying my bachelorhood," Maurice lied.

"Well, I hope so. I gotta have a partner in crime to run with. There are simply too many females out there for me to keep up with." Jamal grabbed his crotch for emphasis.

"But have you ever thought about just finding that special one?" Maurice asked.

"Nigga, please! What the hell's gotten into you? There's no special *one* out there for me. I'll be a player 'til my dying day."

"Well, that's where we differ, homeboy. When the time is right I'll settle down and do the right thang. You know I gotta have a little Mo running around one of these days."

"Listen to you. You sound like that old man you're always talking to. What's his name?"

"Who? Simon?"

"Yeah, sounds like he's gotten into that head of yours. I ain't mad at you, though. Gotta do whatever makes you happy, and getting pussy makes me happy!" Jamal laughed.

"Well, there's more to life than just money and pussy."

"Yeah, like mo' money and mo' pussy."

Maurice ignored Jamal. "I feel like I'm ready for a change. I'm not getting any younger."

"Man, you ought to stop listening to that old fool."

"He's no fool. He's a wise brotha who has a lot to say. Maybe you should come down there with me and pay him a visit one day."

"I *know* you done lost your mind."

"I'm serious, bro. He has a lot of things to say."

"I don't know about all that, man. I hear enough shit from Nicole. She's always trying to preach to a nigga."

"Maybe you ought to start listening."

A few moments of silence passed. Maurice knew he'd struck a chord with him because Jamal shut down.

"So tell me something, Mo. Do you think this Ebony chick is *the one*?" Jamal asked inquisitively.

"I don't know about all that, but like I said, she's got my attention. A wise man once told me to stop thinking with my wayward dick and to start growing up and become a real man handling real issues and responsibilities."

Jamal threw his hands in the air and almost dropped the phone. "Oh, so you're kicking out knowledge now?"

"Man, I'm not trying to preach to you. I'm just letting you know what I'm feeling. I'm thinking about focusing my efforts on finding that special someone." *And I might have found her*, he thought.

Maurice was one of the last people Jamal wanted to hear talking about settling down. Lord knows they both had done their share of dirty deeds between the sheets. But Mo was his ace and, if it made him happy, then he had his back 100 percent.

Maurice thought he'd never have a conversation like that with Jamal. They'd both been players for as long as he could remember. But there was no denying the feelings that made him tingle at the very thought of Ebony.

"You wanna head over to Rally's Sports Bar later tonight?" Jamal asked.

"Nah, I'm hooking up with Ebony for dinner this evening."

Jamal shook his head. "See this is where it starts. Next thing you know, you won't be going out at all. She's got you henpecked already."

Maurice was becoming a bit agitated. "Come on, man. Give it a rest."

"All right, but just remember that I tried to warn you."

"Whatever, bro."

Jamal changed the subject. "Check it out. I had some strange shit take place last night."

"Really? What happened?"

"Stacy and I were getting in the car at the club and there was a note left on my windshield."

"A note? From whom?" Maurice asked.

"I don't know, bro. Probably one of those crazy bitches I used to fuck with. It just said that I'll get what's coming to me and that I'm being watched."

"Man, I told you 'bout messing with those crazy-ass women. Sounds like you got one stalking you. Better watch out for those fatal attractions."

"I ain't worrying 'bout them hoes, man. Just wait 'til I find out which one of them left that note."

"Well, you know you got a long list to choose from."

107

"You know this. But I think I'm going to change my diet. Need some more salt instead of all this pepper. I'm tired of kicking it with black women. They're not dishing out the benefits like the white girls. And there's always a lot of drama with them."

"Don't even go there, bro."

"I'm serious. White chicks are always willing to do whatever at the drop of a dime. When I'm with the sistahs, it's all about the dough. They wanna see how much paper you're willing to drop on them."

"Now how you going to disrespect black women like that? Man, you should be worshiping the ground the black woman walks on!" Maurice fumed.

"Fuck all that! I'm going be with whoever treats me like the king that I am, whether she's white, Mexican, Asian, whatever. I'm just saying that the only sistah who's putting it down is Chantel."

"You mean the married woman?"

"Hey, it ain't my fault her man's not dicking her down right."

"What about Nicole? You better open your eyes before you end up losing something good."

"Nicole is just a bug-a-boo." Jamal huffed. "I mean she's cool, but she's just always trying to make me out to be someone I'm not--like her man."

"Yeah, but she's stuck by your ass longer than anyone else."

"That's true, but she knows she can't put a brotha on a leash. At first she just accepted me for being a dog. Now she's just always bitching about my going out all the time."

The doorbell rang while Jamal was trying to make his point. Maurice heard it.

"Hold on, bro. Let me go see who's at the door."

Jamal opened the door and found Nicole standing with her hands on her hips. Her attitude hung thick in the air between them.

"Why haven't you returned my calls?" she demanded.

Jamal rolled his eyes and opened the door to let her in. "I've been busy, boo-boo," Jamal replied while giving her a kiss on the cheek.

"Busy doing what? Still trying to fuck everything that moves?"

"Don't be walking up in my place starting no shit. I'm not in the mood for it."

Maurice could hear the loud squeal of Nicole's voice. He knew Jamal was in for a good cussing out.

Jamal picked up the phone and continued his conversation with Maurice. "I'm back, bro."

"Sounds like you have company. Nicole is 'bout to put that ass in check," Maurice teased.

"You know I have to handle my business." Jamal looked at Nicole's salty expression and talked louder so that she could hear him clearly. "She ain't running anything up in here. I'll holla at you later, player."

"Play on!"

Chapter Twelve

When A Woman's Fed Up

Nicole was pissed off. She paced back and forth, nearly wearing a hole in his carpet. She waited for Jamal to hang up the phone then lit into him.

"I'm sick of this, Jamal!"

"What are you talking about, woman?" Jamal tried to play dumb.

Nicole put her hands on her hips. "Do you mistake me for a fool? You know damn well what I'm talking about."

"Look, if you got something to say then just say it," Jamal urged.

"As a matter of fact, I do have something to say. I've been putting up with your shit for a long time, and I don't appreciate the way you've been treating me."

"And? You know the type of person I am, Nicole. We've had this conversation over a thousand times."

"Yes, we have, and you still won't grow up. When are you going to raise up, be a man, and stop playing all of these boyish games?"

"Woman, I am a man--from the top of my head to the bottom of my feet. You're looking at nothing but pure black man."

Nicole just shook her head in disgust. "I need a real man in my life, Jamal. Someone who I can trust."

Jamal threw his hands in the air. "Look, if it's that much of a problem for you, then why don't you just step? I don't need you."

Nicole stood silent. Tears began to well up in her eyes. "You...don't...need...me?" she stuttered. "After all I've done for you? Now you're saying that you don't need me?"

"You heard right. I don't see why you are always coming around here starting all this drama in the first place."

"You just don't want to hear the truth!"

"Bitch, fuck you!" Jamal snapped.

Nicole's eyes flew open. "Fuck me? *Fuck me?* No, nigga, fuck you!" Nicole yelled. "I'm tired of putting up with your shit, Jamal. I've had all I can stand. You've finally got what you wanted."

"Oh yeah? And what is that."

"Your freedom."

Jamal began laughing. "See, that's what you failed to realize in the beginning. I've always been free. You never had me on lock down, and you know it."

Nicole shook her head. Tears were now streaming down her face. She couldn't understand how someone could be so cold and heartless. She wiped the tears from her eyes and pulled herself together.

"You know what, Jamal. I may not have all the riches and beauty like a lot of bitches you see every night. But the one thing that I do have is heart, and no one can take that away."

"Well, you can take your little two-cent heart and walk straight out that door." He pointed to the door in case she couldn't remember where it was.

Nicole grabbed her purse and stood straight. She wiped away any trace of tears and flicked her hair over her shoulder. She opened the door and turned around. She gave Jamal a pathetic look.

"You're a poor excuse for a man," she calmly said and walked out the door.

Jamal brushed off the comment. "Stupid-ass woman," he mumbled.

Chapter Thirteen

It's Over Now

Maurice looked forward to his date with Ebony that night. He planned to take her to Basil's Italian Eatery; a cozy Italian restaurant nestled along the beach. Maurice usually dined there alone. This would be the first time someone would accompany him to his place of solitude. Ebony seemed like the type of person who would enjoy a relaxing evening of romance and good food.

Maurice sat in his favorite recliner and turned on his Sony 50-inch television. He couldn't wait until football season rolled around again. There were no good basketball games on, so he decided to watch Tiger Woods whip up on a few pissed-off competitors.

While watching Tiger Woods sink a 25-foot putt for birdie, the telephone rang. Maurice looked over at the caller ID to see who it was, but the number was restricted. He picked up his cordless phone anyway.

"Hello?"

"Hey, you!" Carmen chirped excitedly into the phone.

Maurice wrinkled his brow. He wasn't exactly in the mood to chitchat with Carmen again since the only woman on his mind was Ebony, but he played it off. "What's up, Peaches?"

"Not much. Just wanted to hear your voice. So do you miss me?"

"You know I do," he lied.

"Yeah right, you sound like you're just dying to see me," Carmen said sarcastically. "Well, I can't wait until tomorrow."

"Why, what's up tomorrow?" Maurice asked, forgetting the conversation they'd had earlier.

"I'm coming up to Jacksonville, remember? I told you that I'd call you when I'm coming."

Maurice sighed after realizing he'd just put his foot in his mouth. "Oh yeah, tomorrow is Monday."

"So you've forgotten about me already?" Carmen asked.

"Nah, Peaches, I've just been very busy today. You know me; if I don't write it down I'll probably forget it."

"You better not forget about me. I don't know if I can take another man fucking around with my feelings."

Maurice was a little surprised by her tone. "What do you mean by that?"

"I'm just sick and tired of all these games you guys play."

"Do you think I'm playing a game with you?" Maurice asked, wondering if she somehow knew.

"All men play games, but one of these days that shit is going to catch up to y'all."

"Well, my game-playing days are coming to an end."

"At least you're willing to admit it. All you guys are nothing but dogs."

Maurice was becoming agitated by Carmen's brazen attacks on men. He mainly enjoyed her company because of the physical nature of their relationship. But he could do without her constant ranting about how bad men were.

"Yeah, whatever." Maurice moaned.

Carmen knew something was different with Maurice from the way he sounded. Usually when she called, he was excited and happy to hear from her. Today he sounded dry and apathetic.

"So what's going on, Mo?" she asked.

"What do you mean?"

"Come on now, I didn't just fall off the ship. I can tell something is up."

Maurice shook his head. *I guess all women have that sixth sense,* he thought.

"It's just been a long day."

Maurice heard Carmen sigh. "If I didn't know any better, I'd think you didn't want to talk to me."

"I didn't say that."

"You don't have to say it, Maurice. I can tell. You were short with me earlier and now you're acting all weird. So what is it?"

"Nothing."

Carmen hesitated. "I see."

117

A few more seconds of silence fell as neither one of them said a word.

"It must be another bitch!" Carmen blurted.

"Now how you going to come at me like that? You know the nature of our acquaintance. Even if it were another woman, why should it concern you?"

"Oh, so you're a brazen fool now? After all the time we've spent together, you think that it doesn't count for anything?"

Maurice was wondering what part of the conversation she didn't understand. They'd laid down the ground rules for their relationship in the beginning. Now Carmen was acting way out of character, which came as a surprise to him. He thought of the conversation that he just had with Jamal about Nicole and shook his head.

"Carmen, you were the one who dictated how we were gonna roll when we first hooked up. Why you tripping all of a sudden?"

"Things change, Maurice. I know I suggested that we see other people, but I think that was a mistake."

Maurice laughed in frustration. *Women always try to pull that shit*, he thought.

Carmen continued, "I just want to be with you. I think we've known each other long enough, and I'm tired of just having sex. I need something more in my life."

"You mean to tell me that Ms. Independent Woman wants to settle down?"

"Like I said, things change."

"And what's changed, Carmen?"

"We'll talk about it once I get there."

"Talk? About what?" Maurice asked.

"I'd rather wait until we're in person."

"Why can't we discuss it over the phone?"

"Like I said, I'd rather talk in person."

Maurice knew he'd get nowhere fast in an argument with Carmen. She argued for a living as a lawyer, a damn good one.

"Carmen, I'm going to be upfront with you about what's going down with me right now."

"I'm listening."

Maurice wasn't sure how to say it, but he knew he had to give Carmen the boot. Even though he'd done it many times to many women, it never got easier. The only female he wanted to dedicate his time to was Ebony. That meant putting all of the other *asso*ciates out to pasture, especially Carmen.

He thought about lying, but figured Carmen would see right through his game. So he went against rule number one in the player's handbook--he told the truth.

"I met someone, and I think it's important that you and I step away from seeing each other for a while."

"What the fuck?" Carmen yelled. "What do you mean 'step away for a while'? You weren't talking this shit yesterday."

"I'm sorry. It's just that I'm trying to get a few things straight right now."

Carmen's voice took on ghetto girl attitude. Maurice pictured her on the phone rolling her neck and eyes all in one fluid motion. "You're damn right you're sorry! Just like all the rest of these sorry-ass mofos. I can't believe you're even trying to play me like this, Maurice. To think I was really developing feelings for you."

Maurice was startled at Carmen's reaction. He knew she'd be upset, but he didn't expect her to react like she did.

119

After all, their relationship was only sexual, and she was the one who had stepped to him with the offer.

"Like I said, you knew the type of relationship we had."

"The 'relationship we had'? Excuse me? So you're just throwing me to the side? Just like that?"

"No, it's not just like that. I'm sure we could still be friends."

"Nah, screw that. You're so full of shit, Maurice!" Carmen retorted.

"I don't have time for this, Carmen. I'm trying to be as cordial as possible."

"You're one selfish son of a bitch, Maurice. This is not over!" Carmen yelled.

Maurice opened his mouth to speak, but Carmen had already slammed the phone down.

Chapter Fourteen

A Night To Remember

A soft breeze stirred the air along Atlantic Beach. The full moon bounced off the ocean waters creating an elegant display of romance. Maurice and Ebony strolled hand in hand toward Basil's.

Both were dressed in their Sunday best and looked like quite a handsome couple. Maurice wore a black, double-breasted Armani suit that fit perfectly. His favorite pair of Stacy Adams was polished and looking on point. Ebony wore a black off-the-shoulder cocktail dress that commanded the attention of every eye that gazed upon it. It hugged her hips like a second skin and put her immaculate figure on display. The slit along the side revealed her smooth cinnamon complexion. Her hair cascaded in long waves down her back. Striking silver jewelry accentuated her ensemble.

Walking into the restaurant, all eyes were on them. A beautiful Asian hostess greeted them at the door.

"Good evening, Maurice!" The hostess extended her hand.

Ebony noticed that she knew Maurice by name. *Obviously he's no stranger here. I wonder how many dates he's brought here to wine and dine?* she thought.

"What's up, Janet. How are you this evening?" Maurice asked.

"I'm doing good. Just keeping busy working and studying as usual. Only one more year to go until I graduate!" Janet's eyes squinted when she smiled.

"That's good to hear. Just stay in the books and keep pressing forward. I'd like you to meet a very special friend of mine. Ebony, this is Janet. Janet, this is the lovely Ms. Ebony Stanford."

Ebony smiled and extended her hand. "Nice to meet you."

Janet shook her hand. "Nice to meet you also. I was wondering when Maurice was going to bring someone here to dine with him."

Ebony looked at Maurice in surprise. Janet made it seem as if Maurice came to this place by himself all the time. He noticed the look that Ebony gave him and discerned her thoughts. He smiled.

"The usual spot?" Janet asked.

"The usual." Maurice winked.

Janet grabbed two menus and led the way. Ebony followed close behind the hostess. Maurice walked a few paces behind them both, admiring the rear view of the two lovely females. The sway of Ebony's hourglass hips compared to Janet's more petite Asian figure made him appreciative.

Thank God for the black woman, he thought.

Maurice figured he'd better calm down. His nature was beginning to rise as his eyes sent signals to a part of the brain that keeps men in trouble.

They walked out onto the veranda, which was lit by soft candlelight on each table. Ebony was impressed with Maurice's class and taste. She loved the ambiance of the restaurant. Maurice pulled out the chair for her, and she gracefully glided into the seat.

"If you guys need anything, just ask. Your waitress will be here shortly to take your drink order," Janet said.

"Thanks, Janet. Is Anita working tonight?"

"She sure is. I'll tell her that you're here. She'll be your server." Janet handed them their menus and walked off.

"Who's Anita?" Ebony asked.

"She's a very good friend of mine. We go way back since high school. I'd like you to meet her." Maurice grinned.

Ebony returned his smile. "Cool."

"So how do you like it?"

"It's nice, Mr. Smooth Operator. Is this how you woo all of your dates?" Ebony questioned.

Maurice smiled. "Not exactly. Usually I just take them back to my place and we get straight to the wild thang."

They both laughed. Ebony knew he was joking, but she also knew that truth lay in jesting.

"So do you like Italian food?" Maurice asked.

"Actually, it's my favorite. I can make a mean lasagna."

"Say what? Now that's what I'm talking about. Lasagna is my favorite dish!"

"Well, I'll have to cook up a little something for you one day. You know how we Southern girls from Louisiana throw down in the kitchen."

"Yeah, I heard stories about you Louisiana women."

"What kind of stories?"

"I was told to never let y'all cook me spaghetti."

Ebony waved off the comment. "Now you know that's nothing but a myth. You can't believe everything you hear. But we'll see if you eat my spaghetti."

They both laughed. Just then, Anita walked up next to their table.

"What's up, my peeps? How's everything going?" she asked.

Maurice stood and gave her a big hug. "What's up, lil sis? I thought you were off tonight."

"Nah, you know a woman's got bills to pay. So make sure you leave me a good tip!" Anita wiggled her arched eyebrows.

"Nita, I'd like you to meet someone very dear to me. This is Ebony."

Anita and Ebony shook hands.

"Pleasure to meet you, Ebony. It's about time Maurice found someone he could call dear. Since he's becoming all famous, he acts like he don't know nobody." Anita playfully sucked her teeth and rolled her neck.

"Nice to meet you too," Ebony replied.

Anita's extraverted personality showed itself whenever it got the opportunity. She was quite ghetto fabulous, and Maurice was just hoping that she didn't do anything to embarrass him.

"Girl, you must have a serious impact on this man. This has to be the first time he's brought a woman up in here. He's always sitting here all by himself."

"Goodness, woman! You and Janet are just putting a brotha's business in the street tonight."

Ebony stifled a chuckle while Anita kept rattling on and on about how Maurice thinks he's Mr. Big Stuff since his newfound stardom.

"Anita!" Maurice said in a tone louder than the norm. "Can we please just order our drinks?"

"Slow your roll, Mr. All That. I'll take your order."

Ebony giggled at the interaction between them. She knew Anita was embarrassing Maurice, and she loved every minute of it.

"What can I get you to drink, Ebony?"

"I'll have a glass of chardonnay," Ebony said.

"And you, Big Romeo?"

Maurice scowled. "I'll have the same."

"Two glasses of chardonnay coming right up. I'll leave you two lovebirds alone. I'll be back for your entrée orders in a few."

Ebony laughed when she noticed a look of relief on Maurice's face.

"But you behave now, Maurice!" Anita scolded. "Ebony, if he starts to get on your nerves, just let me know. I know how to handle him."

"I'll keep that in mind, girlfriend," Ebony replied.

Maurice just shook his head and smiled. "Glad to see that y'all have bonded."

Ebony winked at him. "So you really mean to tell me that I'm the first woman you've brought here?"

125

"You would be correct. This is my special place, and in order for me to bring someone here she has to be special."

Ebony blushed. "Oh, so I guess I'm special, right?"

"Webster defines special as surpassing what is common or usual, something exceptional. I would say you're someone exceptional, so you fit the definition."

"I can't believe you're quoting from a dictionary." Ebony laughed.

"Why not? It happens to be one of my favorite books."

"Really? If that's the case, then I guess you're special as well. Reading a dictionary for entertainment is something I'd consider unusual."

"So, Ebony, do you have any brothers or sisters?" he asked.

"No, I'm an only child. I sometimes wish I had a sister. I bet it would've been cool growing up with a sibling. But everything happens for a reason, so it's all good." She looked across the table at him with her big eyes.

"That's what my mother always said. But I don't know if I can agree with that. I see so much that happens in this world, and I just can't comprehend the reasoning behind any of it."

Ebony reached over to touch his hand. "God works in mysterious ways. There are a lot of things that just can't be explained, no matter how much you try to figure it out. Just don't lose faith."

Her touch, her words, and her presence seemed to satisfy his total being. She rubbed his hands gently and gave him a smile of encouragement. When their eyes met, both of them knew that this could be the beginning of something special.

Anita barged in and interrupted their moment. "Here are your drinks. You two ready to order?"

"You're right on time--as usual," Maurice griped.

Anita put her hands on her hips. "Don't start with me tonight, Mo. I'll have to spill all the beans and check you right here in front of your date!"

Ebony gave a quick chuckle as she looked at Maurice. She really enjoyed Anita's sense of humor.

"Yeah, Anita, give me the 411 on Mr. Suave!" Ebony said.

Maurice gave her an incredulous look and shook his head.

"I'm just giving him a hard time. You know I have nothing but love for ya." Anita playfully punched Maurice on the shoulder.

"Thanks for all the love. I *really* appreciate it." Sarcasm dripped from Maurice's words. "Can we just order?"

Anita twisted her lips to the side. "I told you don't be rushing me."

"Let me have the usual chicken and fettuccini with extra Parmesan cheese."

Ebony couldn't decide on her entrée. As an avid lover of all the dishes on the menu, she found it hard to choose.

"Everything sounds so good. Um, let me have the five-layer lasagna."

"OK, y'all, I'll be right back," Anita said. She rolled her eyes at Maurice and walked away.

"I can just feel the love between you two." Ebony was enjoying their show.

"Hard to tell, but she's my girl. I know it's difficult being a single parent, so I try to help out when I can."

127

"She's a single mom?"

"Yeah, she has an adorable 6-year-old son named Malik. I take him out at least every other week. His father's not around and I know how that is, so we hang out a lot."

"Aw, Maurice, that's so sweet."

"Hey, they're our future. If I don't step up to the plate, then who will? You know the black male is considered an endangered species."

"Tell me about it. There are so many lonely sistahs out there because most of the brothers are either locked up or dead. And the remainder are either with a white woman or gay."

Maurice leaned in to emphasize the point he was about to make. "Well, this man is none of those things."

Ebony's cheeks turned hot. "I take it you like kids?" she asked, quickly changing the subject.

"Nah, I don't like kids, I *love* them. Hopefully someday I'll have a little rugrat. He'll be a terror out on the gridiron, making moves that would have Terrell Davis looking like Jamal Anderson after knee surgery."

"Sorry to bust your bubble, but what if you had a girl?"

Maurice's smile turned into a slight frown. "She'd have all of my love as well, but she'd definitely be into sports."

"I feel sorry for the girl already. I can see you taking away her leotards and trading them in for a helmet and pads."

"Who knows, she could be the first female to play in the NFL, dodging tackles and making grown men look like fools," Maurice joked.

Ebony shook her head. "Doesn't sound likely."

"But ultimately my goal is to someday open a youth center focused on the performing arts and sports. Something to get the kids off the streets and away from the television and into creative and athletic pursuits."

"My, my. Impressive goal."

"So what about you? Do you ever want to have children?" Maurice asked.

Ebony turned her head and suddenly became interested in the view of the ocean.

Maurice sensed her hesitation. "Is something wrong?" he inquired.

Ebony refocused her attention on Maurice and gave a faint smile. "No, I'm OK."

"You sure?"

Ebony nodded. She exhaled deeply. "I'm not sure if this is a good idea, but I feel like you're someone who I can talk to."

Maurice observed her serious nature. "Well, you already know I'm a shrink," he joked.

"Please don't think less of me after saying this."

Maurice reached across the table and took her hand. He didn't know what was wrong, but he wanted to let her know that everything would be just fine. "I'll never think less of you—never."

Ebony swallowed the lump in her throat and cast her misty eyes downward. "I...I can't...have any children, Maurice. I'm a barren woman."

Maurice caressed her cheek with one hand. Just seeing her near tears played with his emotions. He didn't want to see her hurt in any way. At that moment, he felt that it was his responsibility to do anything to make sure that she was happy.

129

"It's all right, Ebony." He wiped away a tear that threatened to roll down her cheek.

Ebony smiled at him. "Thanks, Maurice."

"No, I should be thanking you. Thank you for talking to mc. Thank you for letting me take you home last night. Thank you for coming out to dinner. Thank you for coming into my life."

Ebony was too overcome with emotion to utter any words.

Anita walked up to their table with their entrées. "Dinner is served, love birds." She noticed the mood at the table and withheld her usual jokes. "You guys enjoy!"

"Thanks, Nita. Hey, how's my homeboy Malik doing?" asked Maurice.

"He's doing fine. He's over at his cousin's house for the weekend."

"Tell him I said what's up."

"I'll do that when I pick him up tonight. He's looking forward to hanging out with you on Saturday," Anita said.

"Me, too. Can't wait to chill with my little man."

After Anita left, Ebony turned to Maurice. "Sounds like you'll be babysitting on Saturday."

"Yeah, I promised to take Malik to Chuck E. Cheese's. You know how kids are when they hear the name Chuck E. Cheese. That should be the perfect place for him to run wild."

Ebony's spirits brightened. "I'd say. Sounds like fun."

"Really? So clear your calendar for Saturday and join us. We'll roll around in the ball pit and watch the guy in the mouse costume scare the hell out of all the rugrats."

Just the thought of Maurice and her going out with kids made her heart jump. "I think I have a photo shoot scheduled for Saturday, but I'll call and let you know for sure by Wednesday." Ebony paused and took a bite of her food. "Mmm, this is good."

Maurice smiled as he watched Ebony chew her food. What was this woman doing to him? She possessed all of the qualities that he looked for in a woman. Ebony scored a 10 in the beauty department, but she also possessed intelligence, ambition, kindness, and class. Something told Maurice that he'd be turning in his player card soon.

They continued eating and conversing, both probing deeper and deeper into each other. The night was getting late, and they both were ready to leave. Maurice raised his hand and gave Anita the sign for the check.

She came over to their table smiling. "I hope you guys enjoyed your dinner."

"It was lovely, Anita," Ebony replied.

"It was a pleasure meeting you, Ebony. Now don't be a stranger." Anita poked Maurice with her elbow.

"You don't have to worry about that," Maurice said.

Maurice paid the check, and they said their goodbyes. They strolled to Maurice's car. His Raymond Weil timepiece read a few minutes to ten o'clock.

"Damn, time sure does fly by when you're having fun," he said.

Ebony nodded in agreement. "You got that right. And by the way, thanks so much for dinner. It was delicious."

"Anything for you, my angel." Maurice smiled.

"So I'm your angel already?"

Maurice broke into an impromptu performance of "Angel" by Shaggy.

Ebony laughed at the sight of Maurice turning in circles with his arms open and singing slightly off key.

131

"You're something else, Maurice."

He stopped singing and stood in front of Ebony. "If you only knew."

"I think I'm willing to find out."

Maurice took Ebony into his arms. They embraced and shared a long, deep kiss.

Ebony's heart was beating so fast that she thought it was about to jump right out of her chest. She could feel her palms perspiring. After they finished kissing, they stared at each other for a brief moment. Ebony was the first to speak.

"Well, the night's still early. What's next, Horn Boy?"

Maurice smiled. "Would you object if I asked you back to my place? I promise I won't bite."

"I'm not sure if that would be a good idea."

"Why not? We're both consenting adults, and I think you know I wouldn't try anything that you're not comfortable with." Maurice gave her his best puppy dog impression.

"And how do I know that?" Ebony teased.

"I promise I'll be the perfect gentleman."

Ebony put her hand on her chin. "We can go back to your place, but only if you promise me a solo saxophone performance." She licked her lips provocatively.

Oh, you'll get a performance all right, Maurice reflected.

Chapter Fifteen

Let's Get It On

Maurice and Ebony's fingertips were intertwined as they walked up to his condo. They giggled and acted like honeymooners. Once at the door, Maurice turned to Ebony and smiled.

"Ladies first." He opened the door to usher Ebony in.

She blushed. "You're such a gentleman."

"Hey, I try."

Maurice watched in slow motion as this sensuous diva strutted into his home. Ebony pranced in as if she were at home.

Though Maurice had gone through the same routine with many women, there was something about Ebony that gave him goose pimples. She just seemed to light up everything she touched.

Ebony was impressed when she walked into Maurice's bachelor pad. It was very nicely decorated and very clean, which was a good thing. Ebony had a pet peeve about dirty homes.

Looks like the music business is good, she thought.

The décor looked as if a professional had a hand in it. The living room was colored in warm earth tones. The plush carpet was a creamy beige color that made you want to lie down and cuddle. Exquisite pieces of black art covered the wall, each piece matching perfectly with the room. One wall was dedicated to pictures of some of the great jazz legends: Bird, Coltrane, Miles. In the corner of the living room sat a baby grand piano and a few saxophones. Near the sliding glass doors hung a huge ancient African mask. Ebony curiously walked over and studied the relic.

"This doesn't look like something you'd pick up at the flea market."

"That's a mask from the Zulu tribe of South Africa. I was doing a little shopping in Cape Town a few years ago," Maurice replied.

"South Africa? Sounds like you're rather well traveled."

"I manage to do a little traveling from time to time. South Africa was something to remember. That's when I toured with the Jazzmatazz All-Stars."

"Yeah, I bet it was," Ebony said.

"Make yourself at home, sweetie."

Ebony took a seat on the lush leather couch. "Your condo is beautiful."

"It's aw'ight. Gotta have a place to call home."

134

Ebony wondered where Maurice got the money to afford such a setup. She knew most musicians were usually broke and starving, unless they had a major label deal.

Maurice picked up the remote control to the stereo system and pressed play. The jazzy tunes of Paul Taylor engulfed the room. The surround sound speakers made it sound as if they were at a live performance.

Ebony began to make herself comfortable as she relaxed on the couch.

"Can I get you anything to drink?" Maurice asked.

"Just a glass of water. I think I've had enough alcohol for one night."

"You only had a few glasses of chardonnay."

"That's all I need. Trust me, you don't want to see me drunk."

"I'm sure that's a funny sight."

"That it is."

"Aw'ight, I'll get you a glass of water."

Maurice walked into the kitchen, poured a glass of water, and added a slice of lemon. Meanwhile, Ebony walked over to the mantle to look at a few pictures that had caught her eye. Maurice had a lot of pictures from his marching band days.

"You didn't tell me you were so cute when you were young," Ebony said with a laugh.

Maurice yelled from the kitchen. "So what'cha saying? I'm not cute now?"

"Not as cute as you were in these pictures. Oh Lawd, look at those big-ass ears!"

Maurice walked back into the living room and handed Ebony her glass of water. "Now don't you start something you can't finish."

"Oh, I can finish it."

"Don't make me start ranking on you, with your melon head. Got me thinking 'bout spitting watermelon seeds," Maurice joked.

"No, you didn't! You're the last one to talk with that peanut head of yours. I'm afraid to kiss you on the forehead 'cause I might want to add salt and take a bite."

They both laughed. Ebony came across a picture of Maurice and an older woman. She immediately noticed the resemblance.

"Is this your mother?" she asked.

"Yeah, that's Mom. We took that picture a long time ago when we were on vacation in Panama City."

"She's beautiful," said Ebony.

"Yeah, good thing I didn't have a sister. I would've had to fight to keep the boys off of her."

"I know you miss her."

"Yeah, I miss her very much. But let's not talk about that right now," Maurice suggested.

"I understand."

The classic Jodeci slow jam "Forever My Lady" came on.

Just in time, Maurice thought. "Let's dance," he said.

"Only if you promise not to feel on my booty," Ebony announced with a chuckle.

"Are we gonna have to go through that again?" He grabbed Ebony around the waist, and her arms reached up to clasp around his neck.

Maurice was stimulated by the sensual fragrance of her Jean Paul Gautier perfume. The scent played tricks on his sense of smell when Ebony laid her head on his shoulder.

They danced slowly and seductively, Maurice memorizing her curves with his hands. Not a word was spoken for the next five minutes. They just seemed to lose themselves in each other's arms. After the song finished, Ebony looked up at Maurice. "I thought I was going to get a saxophone solo performance?"

"You ain't said nothing but a thang." Maurice released her. He walked over and picked up his tenor sax. "So what would you like to hear?"

Ebony smiled. "Anything you play is fine with me." She was turned on by the way Maurice looked holding his instrument. She found it so sexy.

Maurice led her to the couch and sat next to her. He blew into the sax and it sprang alive from its sleep. He played "Forever My Lady."

Ebony had déjà vu as Maurice serenaded her. But this time there was no crowded club; it was just the two of them. She had him all to herself and relished every note played.

Ebony stood and positioned herself in front of him. Her hypnotic hips began to sway from left to right in sync with his music. Maurice's manhood was now totally attentive. Ebony noticed the bulge in his slacks and smiled.

"Looks like somebody is happy to see me."

Maurice winked and blew harder into the saxophone.

Ebony put her hands on her thighs and began to rotate her hips seductively. Her fingertips pulled her dress to her upper thighs. She could feel the moistness saturating her thong panties. She continued to dance.

She reached over and grabbed the glass of water sitting on the coffee table and pulled out an ice cube. With her body feeling as if it were on fire, she took the ice and sucked it softly, her tongue making circles around the glistening cube.

137

Maurice was enjoying the little show and even missed a few notes, especially when she broke out the ice. Ebony's heart was beating double time and, from the look on her face, Maurice knew the time had come. He abruptly stopped playing the instrument and laid it on the couch. Maurice rushed over to Ebony and took her into his arms. Their passion was now beginning to manifest itself.

Both of them found it hard to control themselves as they kissed deeply. They began removing their clothes as quickly as possible. Maurice removed his shirt and pants almost in one motion as if he'd performed the move a million times.

He then moved around behind Ebony so he could unzip her dress. By this time, he only had on in his boxer briefs and held a bulge that would've made a lesbian moist. He kissed Ebony on her neck and she flinched when his lips touched her sensitive spot. As he continued to kiss her neck, his hands gently caressed her breasts.

Maurice unzipped her dress and it fell to her ankles. Moments later her bra and thongs joined the expensive black dress. His eyes devoured her, and he licked his lips. Ebony was all that he hoped she would be. The fantasy of seeing her naked couldn't compare to the reality of what he was now looking at.

Damn, now this is what I call fine, he thought.

He took his briefs by the waistband and eased them down. They both stood naked and exposed.

Ebony likewise was overcome with mutual attraction as she finally got to see Maurice in his totality.

Maurice scooped her up into his arms. They continued kissing while he carried her into his bedroom. He laid her on the bed and took a moment to admire the beauty that lay before him.

Beginning with soft pecks on her neck, he began to slowly kiss and caress her. Ebony's fantasy of Maurice using his lips to comfort her body was now becoming a reality.

Maurice maneuvered his way down and began kissing her from the bottom of her feet. He placed his warm mouth around her cute toes and licked them one by one. Her breathing increased as she closed her eyes and gripped the satin sheets.

Maurice's probing tongue slowly ventured to her calves, where he gave her a soft bite. Ebony's aching mound was now soaked with her love juices from the anticipation of what was to come. Ebony could feel her body entering a zone.

His tongue slowly circled her knee as he made his way up to her thighs. He felt the warmth emanating from between her thighs.

Ebony opened her legs wider, a sensual ache rising from her pleasure center. Her head was spinning from the intense pleasure she was feeling at that moment. She felt as if her entire body just wanted to explode. Maurice took a moment to admire her nature's beauty, which now stared him in the face. He looked up at Ebony. Her eyes were closed, and she was softly cooing. His tongue led a path directly to her middle.

Ebony squirmed and squealed as Maurice's tongue penetrated her. Moans of ecstasy slipped from her lips.

"Oooh!" She arched her back from the intense pleasure. "Right there, baby!"

She grabbed the back of his head and pulled his face into her even more. She ground her love box against his mouth. Her moans increased when his tongue thrust deeper. Her legs began to weaken.

139

"Right there, baby! Shit, right there!" Ebony screamed, her breathing was now in short rhythmic beats, and her lips puckered like a goldfish.

"Maurice, I'm coming!" She gasped for air. Her legs began to shake violently. Her entire body began to spasm from the extreme pleasure she was experiencing.

Maurice arose and continued on his journey of carnality. His tongue drew circles around her belly button. The satin sheets were now dripping wet with a mixture of sweat and love juices. His tongue found the valley beneath her breasts, while he slowly teased her sensitive spot with his fingers. Her nails were now digging into his back, and she continued to moan.

His warm mouth collapsed around her right areola and he gently bit her nipple. Ebony let out another gasp as he continued to massage her other breast. Ebony arched her back from the sensations she felt. Maurice moved his lips from her breasts and showered luscious kisses on her mouth.

After minutes of sensual kisses, Ebony maneuvered her body on top of his. It was now her turn to take control of the scene, and she wasn't shy about showing him who was really running things.

Ebony took hold of Maurice's hardened penis. "Now how'd this happen?"

"It's all your fault," Maurice teased.

Ebony began to softly caress his dick with her hand. She lowered her head and took him into her mouth. She sucked him slowly and gently. She savored the taste of this black knight who had suddenly walked into her life. With slow and long strokes, she pleasured Maurice until she noticed his toes curl.

"Damn, girl!" Maurice winced.

After some more oral pleasure, Ebony looked up at Maurice and smiled.

"Come on, big daddy. It's time to wrap that thing up."

Maurice reached over into the nightstand next to the bed and pulled out his box of trusty Trojans. He donned his protective raincoat, and Ebony straddled him. She slowly lowered herself down onto his erection.

Maurice shivered briefly from the warmth and moistness he felt when he entered her. Ebony began to ride him with long slow strokes.

"Ooh, damn." Ebony closed her eyes.

Maurice placed his hands on her breasts and played with her nipples. Ebony threw her head back and began to increase her pace. She rotated her hips and bounced up and down. Both of them were now sweating profusely. Ebony's legs began to shudder, and they continued to please each other.

After a few moments of playing cowgirl, Ebony stopped bouncing and detached herself from Maurice. He opened his eyes and looked at her strangely. She stood up from the bed and walked over to the wall. She spread her hands and legs like she was being arrested. Maurice jumped from the bed and followed her. She stood on her toes, arched her lower back, and hiked her butt up. Maurice then entered her from behind.

He must've hit her G-spot because she began to quiver and squirm after only a few strokes.

"Ooh, right there, baby! Right there!" Ebony squealed when Maurice increased his strokes once again. After a few minutes of sexing in her favorite position, Ebony could feel her body climaxing. Maurice sensed that she was near orgasm so he increased the intensity and depth of his strokes until they came simultaneously.

Chapter Sixteen
The Morning After

The next morning, Maurice woke up with Ebony lying across his chest holding onto him tightly as she slept. He wanted to pinch himself to make sure that he wasn't dreaming. Last night was the best night he'd had in a very long time. After sexing a multitude of women in the same bed, this was the first time it actually meant something to him. The fusion of passion was so thick that it left a residue of sensuality lingering throughout the room.

Spring morning showers turned into a vengeful thunderstorm as the rain came tearing down from the sky. Hearing the sound of rain pounding the ground made his bladder tighten and scream for morning relief. Maurice gently lifted Ebony's arm from around his chest and slid from under her, trying his best not to wake her from her peaceful sleep.

He stood next to the bed, staring at her. She lay across his satin comforter in only her sweet chocolate birthday suit, revealing every inch of her brown sugar from head to toe. She was the most eclectic spirit he'd met in years. Even though Ebony was a beautiful woman, Maurice could tell that her beauty ran far more than skin deep.

He bent down and gave her a soft kiss upon her forehead. There was just something about Ebony that he couldn't put his finger on. But whatever it was, he liked it.

Yawning and still trying to rub sleep from his eyes, he headed to his chamber of solitude: the bathroom. His bladder felt as if it was about to burst. Maurice straddled the porcelain toilet and began to let out last night's chardonnay. Once again, he had a little too much to drink.

After peeing for what seemed like an eternity, he walked to the kitchen to see if there were any eggs left in the refrigerator. He figured breakfast in bed would get the day off to a good start, not to mention score some brownie points with Ebony. Just as he opened the refrigerator, the doorbell rang.

Who the hell can that be this early in the morning? he thought.

He wasn't expecting any company, so he figured it probably was Jamal making one of his unannounced visits. He went to his room to retrieve his robe and house slippers and hurriedly put them on. He walked up to the door and looked through the peephole.

Maurice cringed at the sight on the other side of his door.

"Oh shit!" Maurice took a deep sigh.

"Open this damn door!" the voice yelled. "I know you're in there. I can see you looking through the peephole."

Maurice stood motionless, adrenaline being forced into his heart at an alarming rate. Moments passed as he gathered himself together.

He cleared his throat. "Just a minute."

He took another look through the peephole, just to make sure his eyes weren't deceiving him. But sure enough, Carmen stood there soaked from the storm. But it didn't compare to the storm that Maurice knew was about to take place with Carmen.

She was livid, her eyes filled with anger. Her hair was wild, and her hands rested on her hips. Maurice knew he was in for a good cussing out.

He then made a quick run back into the bedroom to make sure Ebony was still asleep. He knew she'd be tired for days after the way he laid the pipe to her, but he didn't want to chance it. Ebony was still laid across the bed and sleeping heavily.

Maurice hurried back to the door and made sure the chain latch was attached. He then opened the door slightly.

"Carmen, what are you doing here?"

"You bastard! I'm still pissed off that you played me like that. I'm not your dirty laundry that you just throw away when you feel like it." Carmen had her defense attorney face on.

Maurice didn't want to get into an argument with Carmen, especially with Ebony in the bedroom. The last thing he needed was for Ebony to wake up and find him arguing with some woman at the door.

"It's not like that, Peaches."

"Bullshit! And don't you 'peaches' me, motherfucker! That's all you niggas are about, nothing but bullshit. I can't believe I even put up with your sorry ass."

Maurice wanted to just shut the door in her face, but he knew if he did that, Carmen would probably end up screaming and acting a fool. So he tried using a more diplomatic approach.

"I'm sorry for all this, Carmen. Really, I am. Let's get together later to talk." He smiled to soften his words.

"Why can't we talk right now? You must have your little bitch in there with you, huh?"

Maurice was beginning to lose his patience. Enough was enough, but just before he was getting ready to explode, Carmen continued.

"Maurice, I'm pregnant, and I'm keeping the baby."

He stared at Carmen, trying to comprehend what she had just said. "You're what?"

"That's right! You heard me, nigga! I said I'm pregnant!"

Maurice didn't know how to respond. "What's that got to do with me?"

"Oh, it has a whole lot to do with you and Mr. Johnson down there." Carmen pointed between Maurice's legs. "I'm two months, and you're the only man I've been with this entire year."

"But we used protection every time we had sex."

"I know, but I'm still pregnant. Condoms aren't 100 percent effective."

"I don't recall having one bust. I don't know what you're talking 'bout," Maurice retorted.

Carmen now had tears welled up in her eyes. "You're the only man I've been with!" she repeated.

Maurice didn't want to believe her. After all, she was dating other men in Orlando. There was no way to know if the child was his right off the bat.

"What, am I supposed to just take your word for it?"

"Fuck you, Maurice!"

The sinking feeling of Carmen being there had now turned into a feeling of being downright nauseous. More silence fell as they both stood staring at each other.

"When did you find this out?" Maurice asked.

"I found out yesterday. I'd been sick and throwing up for days, and I finally took a home pregnancy test."

"Now isn't the time to discuss this. I'll call you later today."

Carmen looked down, her chin touched her chest, and she began shaking her head slowly. "So that's how it's gonna be, huh?" she sniffled. "I don't need you, Maurice. Or should I say, we don't need you!"

Before Maurice could respond, Carmen turned and ran down the hallway crying.

"Carmen!" Maurice yelled, but she didn't respond as she continued to run away.

Maurice closed the door and rested his forehead on the wall of the foyer. He knew sooner or later that his promiscuity would catch up with him. It was moments like this when he pictured his mother looking down on him in shame.

Maurice walked back toward the bedroom, expecting Ebony to be standing next to the door waiting for him to explain himself. But as he opened he bedroom door, he was relieved to see that she was still lying in the exact same position on the bed, still sleeping heavily.

That was a close one, he thought.

Maurice was in the kitchen cooking a gourmet breakfast. He figured he'd show off some of his skills in the kitchen, which seemed to impress most women. He needed to do something to help take his mind off Carmen and the situation he was faced with. He decided right then and there that he wasn't going to stress over this thing. He continued throwing down on ham and cheese omelets, bacon, toast, and grits.

After Maurice finished cooking, he loaded breakfast on a tray and headed to the bedroom. He was amazed to see that Ebony was still asleep. He sat the tray next to the bed and sat down next to her. He kissed her shoulder, his tongue slowly tracing a path to the middle of her back. She slowly woke from her comatose state.

"Hey, what are you doing?"

Maurice smiled and winked at her. "I want my breakfast," he teased while biting her butt.

"You're crazy."

Maurice drew back like he smelled something bad. "Oh, you have the dragon breath this morning."

Ebony got right in his face. "Yeah, but you know you like it," she chuckled.

"You got that right, baby."

They began kissing. Ebony could smell the aroma of the breakfast that Maurice had just cooked.

"What's that smell?" she asked.

Maurice reached down next to the bed and picked up the breakfast tray. "Just a little something I made for you"

Ebony's face lit up like a toddler opening presents on Christmas. "Oh my! Now this is a first. You're the first man who's given me breakfast in bed."

"Well, I guess there's a first time for everything."

They fed each other breakfast and didn't leave a crumb behind on their plates. After they finished eating, they showered together, lingering in the steaming water for a half-hour. They took turns soaping down and washing the other. They both played like little kids in the shower, showing tidbits of affection. After their wet playtime, they dried off and applied lotion to each other.

While Maurice was getting dressed, he noticed he forgot to turn on his cell phone when he woke up. He didn't want to be disturbed during his time with Ebony, so he shut off his cell and turned off the ringer on the house phone.

When he turned on his cell, he noticed he had a few missed calls and a message. He called to check his voice mail.

You have one new message.

Message received at 3:30 a.m.:

Maurice, where are you? This is Anita. Give me a call

when you get this message. It's an emergency!

Maurice looked over at his clock, which read 8:17 a.m. "Damn, let me give her a call and find out what's going on," he mumbled.

Maurice smiled at Ebony and licked his lips, while observing her getting dressed. Ebony smiled back.

"What'cha looking at?" She smirked.

"The most beautiful woman in the world."

149

Maurice dialed Anita's cell number. He wondered what kind of emergency it was this time. After a few rings, Anita answered her phone.

"Hello?"

"What's going on, girl?" Maurice asked.

"Maurice? Where have you been? I've been trying to reach you all morning."

"I had my phone off. Why, what's up? Is everything all right?" Maurice heard the concerned tone of her voice. It sounded as if she was crying.

"I'm down at the hospital with Malik. He fell from the staircase last night!"

"What?" Maurice yelled. "What hospital are you at?"

"University Medical Center."

"I'll be right there!" Maurice hung up the phone.

Ebony sensed that there was an emergency when she heard the word hospital. She walked over to Maurice.

"What's wrong?" she asked curiously.

"Malik is in the hospital. Anita said he fell down the stairs," he replied. Maurice quickly ran into the closet and grabbed a pair of jeans and a T-shirt.

"I'm going with you," Ebony said, pulling her dress back on.

Maurice grabbed his keys. "All right, let's go!"

Maurice shuddered at the thought of anything happening to Malik. That little boy was his heart. They jumped into his car, and Maurice floored it. Ebony sat quietly in the passenger seat as Maurice weaved in and out of lanes along I-95.

"Damn, I hope he's OK," he whispered.

Ebony noticed that Maurice's hands were shaking. She knew he cared for this child like his own. Ebony reached over to stroke Maurice's hand. She gave him a comforting smile. "It's going to be OK, honey."

Maurice felt at ease. Her touch helped to soothe his anxiety.

They arrived at the hospital in what seemed like minutes. Looking for a parking spot in the visitor lot was a nightmare, so Maurice parked next to the curb. He and Ebony hurried into the hospital.

The emergency room was packed with people. Maurice felt like he was watching a scene from *ER* as all of the doctors and nurses walked around in organized chaos. Babies were crying and a few people were arguing with a loud-mouthed nurse. Maurice and Ebony walked up to the receptionist's desk. The phones rang constantly as the woman behind the desk tried her best to answer them.

"Excuse me, I'm trying to find Malik Weber. He was admitted last night."

The receptionist began typing on her computer as she continued to talk into her mouthpiece. She looked back up at Maurice and Ebony.

"He's in Room 404. The elevators are down the hall on the left."

"Thanks," Maurice and Ebony said in unison.

The receptionist continued answering the beeping lines that lit up her telephone console.

Maurice hated hospitals. He'd spent more than enough time in the hospital with his mother when she was going through her chemotherapy sessions. The long corridors and antiseptic smell brought back memories that he'd tried daily to forget. They made it to the fourth floor and walked down the corridor glancing at the numbers on the doors.

"Here's 404," Ebony yelled.

Maurice opened the door and there was Malik lying in bed sound asleep. His little leg was wrapped in a cast, and his arm was in a sling. Anita sat at his bedside. Her eyes were puffy and swollen, giving the obvious sign that she'd been crying all night. When she saw Maurice and Ebony, her eyes widened.

"I'm so glad you guys were able to make it." Anita walked over and embraced them.

"How's he doing?" Maurice asked worriedly.

"The doctor said he'd be just fine. But they had to keep him overnight for observation and some additional tests just to make sure there were no internal injuries."

Maurice breathed a sigh of relief. "How did this happen?" he asked.

"I was in the kitchen washing dishes and Malik was playing upstairs like he usually does. All of a sudden I heard a loud thump and then moaning. I ran out the kitchen and found him lying on the floor near the stairs."

Maurice shook his head. "Did he fall down the stairs?"

"No, he fell from the top floor. He must've been climbing on the railing upstairs."

"I've had to tell that boy so many times to stop climbing on things," Maurice ranted.

"Well, thank God he wasn't seriously injured. When I got to him he was nearly unconscious, so I called 911." Anita sobbed. "I was so scared, Maurice."

Ebony held Anita in her arms. "It's going to be all right, sweetie." Ebony handed her some tissue.

"Thanks, you guys," Anita replied.

"Well, it doesn't look like we'll be making that trip to Chuck E. Cheese's this weekend," Maurice said.

"He was looking forward to that too. Couldn't stop talking 'bout that big old mouse."

They all chuckled as the mood in the room lightened up. Malik's nurse walked in during their laughter.

"Maurice! I thought that was you," the nurse said.

"Nicole! What a surprise. How're you doing?" Maurice replied as he walked over and gave her a hug.

"Not bad, just working hard as usual."

"I didn't know that you worked in the children's ward."

"Yep, this is my beat."

Maurice waved Ebony over. "Ebony, I'd like you to meet a good friend of mine. This is Nicole, Jamal's girlfriend."

"Nice to meet you, Nicole."

"Same here."

"So, Nicole, how's my man Malik doing?"

"He'll be just fine. He took a pretty nasty fall. We're just going to run a few more tests to make sure that he's out of the woods, so to speak."

Anita was relieved and so was Maurice.

"Can I talk to you for a second, Maurice?" Nicole asked.

"Sure."

They walked outside of the room into the hallway.

"What's up, girl?"

"Have you seen your crazy friend lately?" Nicole asked.

"Not since Saturday night at the show."

"I know you and Jamal are close, and I was just wondering if you can just talk some sense into that hard head of his."

"That's a lost cause. I've been trying to talk sense into that boy for a while now."

"I don't know what his problem is. I've been there for him time and time again," Nicole's voice started to break.

"Jamal is my boy and I love him like a brother, but you don't have to take all the mess he dishes out. Move on with your life," Maurice said.

Nicole bowed her head. Her eyes were beginning to become misty. Maurice walked over to her and gave her a brotherly hug.

"It'll be all right, girl. You're a sweet person, and you deserve more than what you have." Maurice didn't want to badmouth his best friend, but he knew he was right. Jamal was nothing but a dog who hadn't grown out of the teenage years.

"Thanks, Mo." Nicole dried her eyes with a tissue from her pocket.

Chapter Seventeen
Living La Vida Loca

With the windows down and his sound system blasting, Jamal cruised down Atlantic Boulevard. He was on his way to Styles, an exclusive clothing store known for the latest urban fashions, to do some shopping. Jamal was still irate from his argument with Nicole the day before. He had a feeling that she was the one harassing him with the threatening note. There was no doubt in his mind after the way she'd acted back at his place Sunday.

Jamal felt his cell phone vibrating at his waist. He turned down the music so he could answer. The caller ID displayed a restricted number, so he didn't know who was calling.

"This is Jamal."

"Hey, big daddy," Chantel spoke.

"What's up, girl?"

"Your dick up in me is what I want," she seductively drawled into the phone. "I'll be all alone next week. Daryl is leaving on deployment again."

Jamal smiled. "You know what that means. I'll be smacking that ass of yours all week long." He laughed.

"You got that right, daddy. I wish I could just have you right now."

"Just close your eyes and imagine I'm right there with you--stroking you just the way you like."

Chantel closed her eyes and began to imagine Jamal inside of her. She put her fingers between her legs and began fondling herself.

"Oh, baby, don't do that. I'm already sitting here wet and horny."

"Good. Just make sure it's still wet next week."

"Little Nina is waiting for you. I was with my husband last night, and it was so frustrating. I can't get no satisfaction from his sorry ass."

"Don't worry about that because it's my job. Just call me the maintenance man."

"Well, I need another tune up. The last mechanic didn't do a good job."

"I'll make sure it's fixed just right."

"That's what I want to hear," Chantel responded. "Well, I have to go get my nails done, so I'll talk to you later.

"Aw'ight then. Give me a holla later when you're free."

"Later, boo."

Jamal laughed after closing his clamshell cell phone. The lack of attention by men gave him a huge pool of women to satisfy, both single and married. Jamal just saw it as equal opportunity loving.

Jamal pulled into the parking lot and blasted his system a little more, hoping to attract the attention of three fly females walking out of a shoe store located next door to Styles. One was wearing a revealing miniskirt with knee high boots, while the other two women were dressed more conservatively. The skirt-wearing female stood out from her peers. Her honey colored hair matched perfectly with her skin tone. From the way she was dressed Jamal knew she was an around the way type of woman.

All of them were wearing sunglasses, so Jamal couldn't tell if they were eyeing him or not. But he knew they'd spotted him when he cranked up the tunes of Tank crooning about how he _deserved_ to be mistreated.

Jamal pulled up next to the car that the women were about to get into. As he stepped out of his ride, he made eye contact with the honey colored beauty in the miniskirt. She slowly removed her shades, obviously to get a better look at Jamal.

"What's up, ladies?" Jamal said, as he approached.

She smiled and quickly put her hands over her mouth. Her face lit up with excitement.

"Aren't you Jamal? The singer with MoJazz?" she beamed.

Jamal loved it when a fan recognized him in public, especially a fan as fine as she. "That would be me. And you are?"

"My name is Monique." She extended her hand.

Jamal took her by the hand and gave it a soft kiss. "Nice to meet you, Monique."

She blushed like a teenage girl at an Usher concert. "Trust me, the pleasure is all mine. I'm a big fan!" She turned and looked at her friends, who were also eyeing Jamal up and down.

"Could I have your autograph?" she asked.

"Of course. Do you have a pen?"

Monique fumbled around in her purse looking for a pen. The only writing instrument she had was a marker.

"What would you like me to autograph?" Jamal asked.

Monique smiled. "How about right here?" She raised the hem of her miniskirt a little and touched the upper part of her thigh.

Jamal took the marker and bent down on one knee to sign his name on her leg. The Calvin Klein fragrance she was wearing began to arouse all of his senses.

"I like that position." Monique chuckled. "Do you like the view from down there?"

Jamal smiled in response. "I like what I see so far."

After he signed his name, he gave her a kiss on the inner thigh. He could feel her legs tremble from the warmth of his lips.

"Ooh, Lawd," she said.

Her friend on the driver's side interrupted them. "Would y'all stop that! Can't y'all see we're in a parking lot?"

Monique turned and gave her the evil eye. "Never mind my friend. She's just jealous."

Jamal stood. They were so close to each other that if Jamal had moved any closer she would've felt the woody in his pants. Monique reached out and grabbed his left bicep.

"You work out a lot?" she asked.

"All the time."

"I do a lot of exercise myself. Maybe we could work out together sometime," she suggested.

"I'd love to work you out. I mean work out with you." He gave Monique a sly grin.

Monique reached in her purse again and pulled out a business card. She handed it to Jamal. "Give me a call later."

"Aw'ight, I'll give you a holla, but don't start nothing you can't finish."

Monique licked her lips seductively. "I've always been a good finisher."

She stepped into the passenger side of her friend's car, and Jamal politely closed the door for her. Jamal knew that she and her friends were about to get into an argument. Her friends didn't crack one smile the entire time they were talking.

As Jamal walked across the parking lot, a black Nissan Maxima sped down the lane. Jamal looked to his left and saw the car come to a screeching halt only a few yards away from where he stood.

"Hey, man, watch where the fuck you're going!" Jamal yelled.

The front window was tinted, so it was hard to see a face through the windshield. Jamal just stared at the driver's side and continued walking. After he stepped onto the sidewalk, the Maxima screeched off. Jamal just shook his head in repugnance.

"Damn crazy-ass drivers, he huffed.

Styles was packed. The store was having its usual first-of-the-month sale, so the place was filled with everyone looking for fresh gear and new kicks.

When he walked into the store he noticed a few women behind the counter laughing and having a good time. The loud sounds of Ludacris shook the walls throughout the store. Once the sales ladies noticed Jamal walk through the door, one of them came from behind the counter.

"Good afternoon, sir. May I help you?" she smiled, looking extremely sexy in her Baby Phat outfit.

Jamal noticed the usual girls still behind the counter, looking at him and smiling. His usual doggish instincts had already begun to kick into overdrive. He'd almost forgotten the reason he'd came to the store.

"Well, that depends." He looked at her nametag. "Margarita? Did I pronounce your name correctly?"

"Yes, you did." She continued to smile. "So it depends on what?" Margarita was a beautiful, full-figured Latina with more curves than the Pennsylvania Turnpike. Jamal stepped back and gave her a look from head to toe.

"Depends on you being available."

Margarita blushed and flung her long straight hair over her shoulder. That's when Jamal knew she'd just let him into her door.

"That's a lovely name. Just like the drink. I'm sure you're just as intoxicating, aren't you?"

"You got that right, papi." Margarita put her hands on her wide hips.

Another around-the-way girl. This is my lucky day, he thought.

"You must be new here."

"Yeah, actually today is my first day working here."

Jamal put his hand on his chin. "I thought so. I come here often to shop, and this is the first time I've seen you."

One of the usual sales associates walked from behind the counter and approached them. "What's up, Jamal?" she asked.

"Hey, Valencia, how are you?" Jamal replied.

"I'm aw'ight, just training our newbie here." She pointed to Margarita.

"Well, I'd recommend her for a promotion. She's doing a *fine* job already." Jamal looked Margarita up and down.

"Mm hmm, I bet." Valencia smiled. "So what can we get for ya today?"

"I'm looking for a new suit."

Valencia turned to her co-worker and gave her a wink. "Margarita, take Jamal over to the suit section and help him pick out something nice."

"I like that idea," Jamal interjected.

"Just watch out for him, Margarita. He's a pro." Valencia smirked. "Trust me, I know."

"I'm a big girl," Margarita replied with a wink. She turned and began walking to the rear of the store.

Jamal followed behind her, his eyes burning a hole through her denim bodysuit. Her outfit didn't have back pockets, and no panty lines were visible. Her well-toned ass mesmerized Jamal. She wasn't fat, but just big boned. All Jamal could think about was fucking this woman silly.

They walked to the suit section. A majority of the customers were up front and only a few lingered in the back where they were. Margarita turned to him and licked her full luscious lips.

"So are you looking for something in particular?" she asked.

161

Jamal looked at her breasts threatening to break free from the haltered top of the bodysuit. "Just something hot, spicy, and sexy, with a Latin twist, of course."

Margarita bit her bottom lip. "I see. I have the perfect thing for you."

She reached over and pulled an eight-button Stacy Adams suit from the rack. Jamal liked the blue pinstriped garment.

"I'm feeling that. Blue happens to be my favorite color." He leaned down to whisper in her ear. "But I like the blue that's on you even more."

Margarita looked around the store. The customers who were in their section had already walked to the counter with their purchases. She grabbed Jamal by the hand, and they walked into the woman's bathroom. Since it was only a one-stall bathroom, Margarita locked the door behind them.

In record time Jamal had dropped his pants and taken out his rock-hard dick. With a quick snap and one long zip from the zipper on her body suit, Margarita stood butt naked; she wore no underwear to bother with. Jamal was amazed at how a woman so big didn't have an ounce of fat on her body. Her full voluptuous thighs were the sexiest he'd ever seen. Her 38DD breasts just sent a tingle through him. Without hesitation Jamal grabbed hold of one of her breasts and began to give it a thorough tongue-lashing. He could tell she was horny as hell because when he sucked one nipple and fondled the other, Margarita was already starting her first orgasm.

Margarita then walked over and put her leg up on the porcelain sink. Jamal quickly reached into his wallet and pulled out his trusty Trojan. He slid it on his shaft and walked over to Margarita. Her ass looked so perfect. She turned around and winked at Jamal as he approached her. She was amazed at his size.

"Damn, papi!"

Her legs were already trembling with anticipation of his long black dick ramming into her from the back. Jamal walked up to her and put all nine and a half inside. Margarita was so wet that he was able to slide all the way in her with one thrust. She gasped loudly at first, but tried to conceal her moans since they were in a public place.

He grabbed her thick waistline and began pounding into this Latin diva with all of his strength. Margarita just bit her bottom lip as she desperately tried to hold back the moans. Jamal got a kick out of her big ass slapping against his abs. Within one minute, Margarita's orgasm began. She pounded her fist on the concrete wall next to the soap dispenser. Her body began to shake and quiver violently. Jamal increased his strokes, and he began to shiver as well. He pulled her hair tightly as they both climaxed simultaneously.

Margarita looked at the watch on her wrist. The entire process had taken only four minutes. It was the most intense four minutes she had ever experienced. She quickly put back on her bodysuit, and Jamal hastily hauled his clothes back on. Margarita ran her fingers through her hair to make sure that it wasn't a mess. She then turned to Jamal as he was zipping his pants.

"You have to come shopping here more often."

"Oh, trust me, I will," Jamal replied.

Margarita was the first to walk out of the door. She quickly walked out from the back and into the suit department. She began straightening a few clothes on the rack and working as if nothing ever happened. A few seconds later, Jamal appeared. He walked over next to her.

"You know what? I think I'll take this blue suit right here."

They proceeded to front of the store where the other ladies were behind the counter giggling. Valencia was grinning from ear to ear.

"So how was your shopping experience today?" she asked Jamal.

"It was good, as usual. You know I have to break in the new hires."

"Yeah, don't I know it." Valencia winked.

Margarita walked behind the counter and began ringing up the merchandise he had just purchased.

"Thanks for *coming* to see us. Make sure you *come* again," Margarita said with a smile.

"I can't wait to *come* back." Jamal grabbed the suit bag and walked out of the store.

Chapter Eighteen
Friends and Lovers

Maurice and Ebony were on their way to Twilight Arms to visit Simon since his Saturday plans with Malik had to be postponed. It had only been a few days, but he finally had a woman who he could introduce to his friend. He only wished that he could bring Ebony home to his mother; he knew they would've loved each other.

Maurice noticed that Ebony was a bit fidgety, as if something was on her mind. He just remained quiet and waited for her to talk. After a few minutes of silence Ebony finally spoke.

"Maurice, can I ask you a question?"

"Go ahead, shoot."

"Who is Carmen?"

Maurice could feel his heart drop to the pit of his stomach. He was totally caught off guard by the question.

"Carmen who?" he replied, trying to play dumb.

"The Carmen who was at your door the other morning. I wasn't trying to pry into your business, but I heard you mention her name. I couldn't make out what you guys were arguing about, but she sounded pissed."

Maurice sighed. "It's a long story."

Ebony readjusted herself in the seat to face Maurice. "I'm a sucker for long stories."

Maurice knew he couldn't keep this from her. He'd been down the road of lies far too many times, and experience had taught him that all dirt comes out in the wash. Maurice wanted to have something special with this woman. He knew the foundation for a good relationship started with honesty.

"Carmen is just a woman I used to kick it with. She lives down in Orlando, but she comes up here to Jacksonville often."

Ebony folded her arms and arched her eyebrows. "So do you still have feelings for her?"

"Nah, baby. It's over between us, even though she doesn't want it to be. Carmen and I were just a fly-by-night fling, and we both got comfortable with our situation."

"Well, pardon my candor, but I just want to make sure I'm not interrupting anything."

"Ebony, you're the best thing that's happened to me in a long time. I think we have something special here and I want to build on that. I've had a lot of women during my day, but those days are gone. I admit I've done it all. But that's not the type of lifestyle I want," Maurice confessed.

Ebony didn't know whether to believe him or not. She was well aware of the games men played.

"I feel the same way, Maurice, but I'm just being careful. I've been down this road so many times."

"I know, sweetie, but I assure you it's nothing to worry about. I don't know why I'm telling you all of this, but I just feel the need to come clean."

"You don't have to explain your past to me, Maurice."

"No, I insist," he replied. "It's not something that I'm proud of, but I've always been a dog since my teenage years. Don't get it twisted, I've always respected women and treated them like queens, but my problem was that I had to have more than one. But I'm done with the game and I'm ready to move forward with my life."

Ebony reached over and touched his hand. "Making the transition from boy to man, huh?"

"I guess you can call it that. I'm not getting any younger, that's for sure."

"I'm glad you realize that, Maurice. It's takes a real man to 'fess up and say what you just did."

"As Jennifer Lopez would say, I'm real."

They both shared a brief chuckle.

"But there's more to the story with Carmen," Maurice continued.

"Oh?"

"The reason she stopped by yesterday--"

Maurice hesitated, wondering if he should tell Ebony about his situation with Carmen. But he wanted to--had to--lay everything on the table. He didn't want to keep any secrets from Ebony. He wanted to gain her full trust instead of digging a hole of lies and deception.

"What is it?"

167

"She stopped by to tell me that she's pregnant, and she thinks the baby is mine."

Ebony didn't know how to respond to the bombshell that had been dropped on her emotions. She became quiet as the mood of their conversation suddenly changed. Ebony turned and looked out of the passenger window.

Noticing Ebony's unresponsiveness, Maurice continued. "And I don't know what to do. I mean, if it's my child then I'll do what's right and take responsibility. But she's dated other men while in Orlando. I don't want to just take her word for it, you know?"

Ebony remained silent as she observed the view out of the window. She appreciated Maurice's honesty, but she still felt uneasy. She didn't like the thought of another woman giving Maurice something that she wasn't able to give him: a child.

Moments of difficult silence engulfed the car as Maurice waited for Ebony to respond. She took a deep breath to steady herself. "I appreciate your honesty, Maurice. I know how hard it is for a man to communicate his emotions like that."

"All I ask is that you trust me. That's why I want to be upfront with you."

She turned to face him. "Well, I'm trusting you, so don't disappoint me."

Ebony had a newfound respect for Maurice. Even though she didn't like the news, she appreciated his candor.

"I won't, baby. I won't." Maurice's heart felt at ease. Ebony knew how to bring calm to the worst of situations.

Ebony changed the subject. "I'm nervous about meeting Simon. I always hear you talking about him and holding him in such high regard."

"You don't have to be nervous. You'll love him. He's cool people."

"I hope so."

Ebony pulled down the passenger visor and looked in the mirror. She began brushing her long black hair and checking her makeup. After she touched up the dark red lipstick on her succulent lips, she turned to Maurice.

"How do I look?"

"Woman, what kind of question is that? You're the best looking gal this side of the Mississippi!" he teased with an exaggerated southern accent.

Ebony chuckled. "You're so crazy."

After battling the traffic going across the Intercoastal waterway, they finally arrived at Twilight Arms. Maurice parked near the entrance. He walked over to the other side of the car and let Ebony out.

Carla greeted the couple at the lobby. Maurice could tell from her expression that she was disappointed. But Carla swallowed her pride and was very cordial.

"Hello, Maurice," Carla said with a wave and a half-smile.

Maurice returned the gesture. "Hey, Carla, how are you this morning?"

"I'm doing as well as can be expected." She walked closer to the couple.

Maurice shook her hand. "I'd like you to meet a very special friend of mine," Maurice beamed. "This is Ebony Stanford."

Carla smiled. "Nice to meet you, Ebony."

"Nice to meet you too, Carla."

"We're on our way upstairs to see what the maestro is up to."

"I think he's up there on the piano. He's been playing that thing all morning long," Carla said. She turned to Ebony. "Girlfriend, be on the lookout for the other guys. They're in rare form today."

"Thanks for the 411. Maurice hipped me to the Viagra Posse," Ebony laughed.

They parted ways with Carla and went upstairs. When Maurice and Ebony walked into the lounge area on the second floor, all of the guys ran up to them.

Clyde whistled. "Looky here, looky here."

"What's up, Mo?" Otis gave Maurice some dap. "Looks like you've finally brought us what we've been asking for." He looked Ebony up and down, licking his ashy lips.

Ebony covered her mouth with her hand and gave Maurice an astonished look.

"Nah, old-timer, this is the love of my life right here," Maurice replied. "I'd like you guys to meet the lovely Ebony Stanford."

Otis laughed. "You in love? Get outta here."

"Yeah, man, I had to turn in that players' card." Maurice grinned.

"Say it isn't so, Mo. Not you!" Otis pleaded.

Clyde was the first to step up and take Ebony's hand. "Nice to meet such a lovely black princess. My name is Clyde Peterson," he said, giving her a soft kiss on her hand.

Otis stepped forward and interrupted him. "Quit licking on the woman's hand before it falls off."

Clyde turned and gave Otis an evil look. "Would you shut the hell up, Otis? I'm trying to talk to the young lady."

Maurice just shook his head. Ebony laughed at the interaction between the two elderly men.

170

"Listen, guys, I'd like to stay around and chitchat, but Simon is expecting us."

"Don't worry bout that, Mo. You go ahead and visit that old geezer, and I'll keep this young lady company." Otis put his arm around Ebony.

"Sorry, old-timer, no can do. I don't want to leave her here with you dogs. Y'all have to get your own bone."

"It was nice meeting all of you," Ebony remarked with a smile.

"Nice meeting you too, Ms. Pretty. Don't be a stranger 'round here." Otis waved and Clyde blew her a kiss.

"I won't," Ebony replied.

Maurice took her hand and led her down the corridor to Simon's room. They could hear the melodic sounds of a piano as they approached Simon's door.

Ebony turned to Maurice. "Sounds good."

"Oh, you haven't heard anything yet." Maurice knocked on the door.

"Come on in!" Simon yelled above the piano.

When Maurice opened the door, Simon was playing the piano with his eyes closed. He was playing a classical piece written by Bach in A minor. Ebony was amazed by what she heard. Simon's hands blissfully glided across the ivory keys, making the piano sing in a tone that sent chills down her spine.

"Damn, he's good!" Ebony whispered to Maurice.

"Trust me, he's not only good, he's the best. It doesn't get any better," Maurice bragged.

After Simon finished the last note, Ebony and Maurice clapped enthusiastically. He bent slightly at the waist and took a bow from his wheelchair.

"That was incredible!" Ebony said.

"Thank you, thank you, sweetheart."

"Hey, Pops, I'd like you to meet the woman I've been telling you about. This is Ebony Stanford."

Ebony reached out to shake his hand, but Simon refused.

"I'm from the old school, Ebony. Come over here and give an old man a hug!" he smiled.

Ebony bent down and hugged him. The smell of Old Spice was undeniable. She was surprised at how handsome Simon was for his age.

"It's good to finally meet the woman who has accomplished the impossible. I thought this boy would never fall in love, but thank God I'm around to see it. What a difference a week makes." Simon chuckled.

"All right now, Pops," Maurice retorted.

"What do you mean 'all right'? The boy has love written all over his face!" Simon laughed. He took a good look at Ebony. "You weren't lying, MoJazz. She is incredibly beautiful."

Ebony blushed. "Thank you. I see I've been a topic of conversation."

"No, my Nubian queen, you've been a top of many conversations." Simon smiled. "Please, have a seat."

Maurice and Ebony took a seat on the couch next to the piano.

"So, Ebony, where are you from?" Simon asked.

"I'm originally from Louisiana."

"Oh yeah. I have a lot of memories from New Orleans. I used to play there way back in the days--when your parents were just a twinkle in your grandparents' eyes," he remembered with a laugh. "I sure miss that place."

Ebony shook her head in agreement. "So, Simon, how about you? Are you originally from Florida?"

"Nah, I'm from the south side of Chicago. I wound up in Florida by chance, but I'd love to go back home one day. I miss it too much."

"I know the feeling. I've been considering taking a trip back to Louisiana. I haven't seen my kinfolk in years. That's if Maurice would be interested in tagging along."

"You ain't said nothing but a thang," Maurice replied.

"Simon, where did you learn to play the piano like that?" Ebony asked.

"I've been dibbling around with this thing since I was knee high to a grasshopper. To tell the truth, I can't remember what inspired me to start playing. I just fell in love with the damn thing."

"I know that feeling. I experienced the same with my camera."

"Well, I guess we all have something in common--a passion for the things we love," Maurice remarked.

They continued to converse about a multitude of subjects. Simon was impressed with the class that Ebony personified. It made his heart sing to watch the lovebirds' affectionate interaction. It didn't take long to convince Simon; Ebony was the woman with whom Maurice would spend the rest of his life.

Chapter Nineteen
Back In Stride Again

Two days had passed since Maurice had last seen Ebony. Even though they conversed on the phone at least three times a day, those two days apart felt like a lifetime. Ebony was extremely busy on location at the Amelia Island Plantation just north of Jacksonville. Chris Tucker was there filming his latest movie, and Ebony was hired as a photographer for the actors' press interviews. She was very excited and would call Maurice throughout the day to let him know how everything was going.

Maurice continued to clean up his condo. He was expecting Ebony in 15 minutes. She'd called him earlier and told him to be ready for a night that he wouldn't forget.

The scene was set, and Maurice was ready to seduce her the moment she stepped in the door. His bedroom was decorated with jasmine-scented candles that were already burning slowly. Rose petals marked a trail from the entrance of the door to the bedroom. The king-sized bed was covered in petals.

Maurice was dressed in his silk Jacquard boxers with matching robe and slippers. His heart beat with anticipation as he anxiously waited his queen's arrival. The doorbell rang just as he was shuffling through his slow jam CD's.

Maurice quickly put in his Luther Vandross greatest hits CD and pressed play. He picked up the bouquet of roses he'd bought, hid them behind his back, and went to open the door.

Ebony could feel her heart skip a beat when her loving prince appeared from behind his door. Their eyes locked, and both of their worlds stood still. Maurice looked at her and couldn't hold back the smile on his face. She was already showing her impeccable one.

She wore a black trench coat with a pair of stilettos. Her hair was pulled back into a bun, giving her an exotic look that made Maurice jump to attention.

"Damn, I'm so happy to see you." Maurice grinned.

Ebony walked up to him and hugged him tightly around the neck. "I can tell," she said as she looked down at the bulge protruding from his boxers.

Their lips met, and Maurice kissed her deeply. He grabbed her petite waist. His hands began to explore her body. Ebony squeezed his neck as she held onto him. Maurice scooped her up into his arms and followed the trail of rose petals into the bedroom while their lips were still locked together.

Once at the foot of the bed, he let her down. Ebony looked deep into his eyes. She then untied the trench coat and let it fall to the floor. She stood in front of him naked and exposed.

"I'm yours," she announced, a mischievous grin lighting her face.

Maurice could feel his heart tingle with emotion. The feelings he experienced at that moment were better than anything he'd ever felt. He disrobed and took off his boxers.

"I'm yours too," he replied.

They stood before each other--the same way it was in the beginning with man and woman. Maurice looked deeply into her eyes. Ebony lay down on the bed of roses. Maurice followed suit and moved on top of her.

The sounds of Luther helped to set the romantic scene. The silhouette of their shadows danced upon the walls through the flickering candlelight as they made passionate love.

After their intense lovemaking, they both lay quietly. Ebony held onto Maurice tightly as she laid her head on his broad chest.

Maurice couldn't understand it, but he felt very vulnerable. Nothing else mattered to him. All he could think about was Ebony. For the first time in his life he'd found something he loved more than music. He continued to stroke her long black hair.

Just before he reached over to turn off the light, he looked Ebony in the eye. For the first time in his life he knew how it felt to love a woman. He did something he thought he'd never do.

"I love you, Ebony Stanford," Maurice uttered sincerely.

Tears began rolling down her soft cheeks almost immediately after Maurice spoke those three words. She'd been waiting a long time to sincerely hear those words from a man. This time she knew she had the real thing.

"I love you too, Maurice LaSalle."

They embraced and fell asleep in each other's arms.

Chapter Twenty

Caught Up

A few weeks had passed, and everything was going well. MoJazz was getting ready to release "Feel the Heat," and it was about to be on.

Maurice and Ebony's relationship continued burning brightly. They could barely stand to be out of each other's presence.

Malik had fully recovered from his accident and seemed to be even more daring than before. Anita had since moved into a one-story home since she didn't want to take any more chances with Malik thinking he was Superman and pulling a fly-by off the staircase.

Maurice hadn't heard from Carmen since she showed up at his door. He tried numerous times to contact her, to no avail. Her phone numbers had been changed, and her secretary intercepted all of his calls.

It bothered him to think that he may have a child who would enter the world and wouldn't be a part of his life. All he wanted was a DNA test to find out if the child was or wasn't his.

Jamal was still the consummate ladies' man, sexing chicks before *and* after every show. Chantel was still fucking him when her husband wasn't around.

Aside from all the sex, Jamal went on and on about how he thought Nicole was stalking him. He found more threatening notes on his truck. After his tires were slashed, his paint job keyed, and the windshield smashed with a cinder block, Maurice pleaded with him to go to the police. Jamal insisted he could handle the "crazy bitch."

It was a Monday morning, and Maurice was at home for some much-needed relaxation. MoJazz had just returned from a weekend promotional tour. It felt good to be home.

Maurice was lounging in his boxer briefs on the couch reading *The Maintenance Man* by Michael Baisden. It was a story about a male gigolo doing his thang. Maurice looked down at his dick and said, "You remember those days, don't you?"

Just as he was getting into a juicy part of the book, the doorbell rang. He put down his reading glasses and went to answer the door.

"Who is it?" Maurice asked while walking toward the door.

A familiar voice answered, "It's Charlene."

Maurice wrinkled his eyebrows. Charlene had never even visited him before, and he wondered how she even knew where he lived. When he looked through the peephole he saw the lovely face of Ebony's best friend. He opened the door, and her perfume wafted over him like a fresh spring breeze blowing in from the ocean. Charlene stood in the doorway with a salacious grin on her face.

She wore a beige sundress that hugged her sexy figure, falling a few inches above her knees. She carried a matching handbag and wore open-toed mules that exposed a lovely set of freshly manicured toes. The dress hung low across her breasts, exposing two large mounds of cleavage. She wasn't wearing a bra, so her attentive nipples peered through the material.

Maurice took a hard swallow and spoke in a near trembling voice. "What's up, Charlene? What are you doing here?" Maurice tried to avoid looking at her exposed chest.

"I was just in the neighborhood and thought I'd drop by to say hello."

Maurice thought to himself, *Just in the neighborhood, huh? Yeah, right.*

"So can I come in?" she asked.

Maurice knew the best thing to do was to just say no, but since Charlene and Ebony were such good friends he figured what the hell. "Sure, come on in," he said, stepping aside.

Charlene strutted seductively past Maurice with her hips switching from side to side. She knew he was looking at her ass and that was her intention. She remembered Ebony telling her that Maurice was fascinated with big butts and cute toes. She possessed both.

Maurice tried his best not to pay any attention, but his eyes were being disobedient. He knew he was in for trouble.

181

"This is a nice place you have here," Charlene noted as she gazed around. "Ebony always talks about how nice your place is."

"Well, it's home for now. I hope to be moving to a much larger place later in the year."

Charlene walked over to the bar and took a seat on a barstool. When she sat down, her sundress climbed up her legs, revealing her voluptuous thighs.

"Can I get you something to drink?" Maurice asked.

She crossed her legs and put her hand on her knee. "How about a glass of chardonnay?" She pointed toward the wine rack behind the bar.

"I guess you and Ebony have a lot in common. That's the same thing she drinks," Maurice said, trying to keep Ebony's name in the conversation. He walked over to the wine rack and removed one of the bottles usually reserved for him and Ebony.

"Yes, we do have a lot in common. We like photography, sports, and good-looking men like yourself." She licked her lips seductively.

Maurice had his back turned to her while he was pouring her the glass of wine, but he could feel her looking him up and down. "That's good to hear, Charlene. You're lucky to have a *best friend* like Ebony," he replied, emphasizing best friend.

He handed her the glass of chardonnay. She took a sip and closed her eyes for a brief moment.

"Yeah, that's my girl. She always gets what she wants."

Maurice could sense the jealousy in her words. This had all come as a surprise to him. He'd known Charlene for a short time, but she always seemed to be cool. Now he was seeing another side of her.

"Have you talked to Ebony today?" Maurice asked.

Charlene took another sip. "Yeah, I talked to her earlier this morning while she was at the studio. She'll be tied up with a photo shoot all afternoon."

"That's my baby, always busy." Maurice smiled.

Charlene just continued to sip on her drink. "Tell me something, Maurice. What would you do if you found out that a person close to you betrayed you?"

The question blindsided Maurice. "Uh, I don't know," he responded, searching for words. "I guess that would depend on my relationship with that person. Either way, I'd still be pissed, especially if it was someone that I'm close to."

Charlene sipped her drink once again. Maurice knew where she was going with the conversation, but he played along.

"Why do you ask?" Maurice asked her.

Charlene waived her hand nonchalantly and downed the rest of her chardonnay in one gulp.

"Oh, it's nothing. Just man problems, that's all. Anyway could I use your bathroom?"

"Sure, it's down the hall on your left."

Maurice knew something was up. He figured he'd confront her and then show her the door when she came out of the bathroom. It was quite obvious that she was trying to make a move on him. That really pissed him off because he knew it would hurt Ebony if she found out that her best friend was trying to get with her man.

He sat on the couch, turned on the TV, and began flipping through the channels. A few minutes went by, and Maurice heard the sound of the toilet flushing. The bathroom door opened, and Charlene walked out. His back was to the bathroom so he didn't see her when she tiptoed into the living room. She crept up behind him and put her arms around his neck.

Startled, Maurice jumped to his feet. When he turned to face Charlene, she stood butt naked with a lascivious look on her face. Her legs were slightly bowed with a nice gap between them. Maurice's jaw nearly hit the floor as he stood there looking at Charlene's stunning figure. His manhood became erect at the drop of a dime.

"What the hell are you doing?" he asked. His voice was breaking up, sounding like he was on an out-of-range radio.

"I'm doing what I should've done a long time ago. You know I've wanted you ever since I laid eyes on you at the track." Charlene walked from behind the couch toward Maurice.

Maurice took a few steps back. "What are you talking about? You're Ebony's best friend! How are you going to even come at me like that? That's foul!"

"I don't care, Maurice. Ebony always gets what she wants; now it's my turn. I see the way you look at me when I'm around." She now stood in front of him. She shoved Maurice down onto the couch.

"Calm down, woman!" Maurice yelled as he scooted down to the other end of the couch.

"I am calm. You should see me when I'm aggressive," she retorted. Charlene grabbed Maurice by his boxer briefs and yanked them down in one motion. Maurice could hear his conscience telling him to pull up his boxers and kick her out, but he was caught up in the lust of the moment.

Charlene grabbed his attentive dick and quickly lowered her mouth onto it. Everything had happened so fast that he couldn't believe what was going on, let alone stop it.

"Charlene, get off--"

Charlene covered his lips with her hand and cut him off in mid-sentence. She began to move her head up and down in quick strokes. Maurice was in an awkward position, but he felt himself responding as she continued doing her dirty deed of seduction. Her technique was unlike anything he'd experienced. His mind was telling his body to resist, but the attempt was futile.

His mind flashed to Ebony. The feeling of pleasure was so immense that he couldn't determine whether he should enjoy the moment or bring it to an end. So he lay there with every part of his body in total contentment, as each second seemed like a minute.

Every time he tried to move, Charlene would deep throat him. Maurice could feel his horniness going to another level. He loved Ebony with all of his heart, but the lust that had reared its head was too hard to walk away from. He reached down and slid his hand between her legs and felt the warm, wet sensation of her pussy. She continued to give him head like a professional. He inserted his finger inside her, and she moaned.

Charlene began to move her body against his hand as if wanting it to find the right spot. She opened her legs wider as her love juices continued to flow. She stopped sucking Maurice and looked up at him.

Charlene turned around and got into a doggy-style position. She grasped the back of the couch firmly, waiting for Maurice to ram into her from behind. Maurice sat there speechless. He looked at the vision of the finest chocolate ass that a man could ever want, staring him right in the face.

But that split second of admiration allowed him to think about Ebony. Maurice didn't want to dip out on her, especially with her best friend. Ebony was the love of his life. Reluctance began to seep in as he stood looking at Charlene.

Charlene sensed his hesitation. She looked back. "What are you doing? You better come get this pussy!" she demanded.

At that point his male instincts took over. Fueled by anger for feeling so helpless, Maurice grabbed her by the hair.

"That's it, daddy! Fuck me hard!"

Maurice spread her beautiful cheeks and was about to slide in when the phone rang. He released his grip as if the phone had awakened him out of a trance.

"Forget the phone! Fuck me now!" she pleaded.

Maurice could feel time stand still as he pondered his next move. The answering machine picked up, and Ebony's voice spoke.

Hey, baby, I was just thinking about you and wanted to let

you know that I love you. Call me when you get this

message.

A blanket of guilt fell throughout the room. Maurice looked at Charlene on all fours waiting for him. Her vagina looked so inviting, but Ebony's voice had awakened him from his lustful stupor. He stepped back and picked up his briefs.

"What are you doing?" Charlene asked.

Anger welled up in Maurice as he looked at Charlene. "You trick-ass bitch, get the fuck out of my house!" he yelled. "I can't believe you'd even try to go there."

Charlene jumped up and got into Maurice's face. "I didn't hear you complaining when I was sucking your dick! You're no better than me! You're a dog, and you know it," she shot back.

186

Maurice ran into the bathroom and grabbed Charlene's clothes. He went back into the living room and threw them at her. "Get the hell out!"

"Fuck you!" she replied as she quickly gathered her clothes. "I'm glad you didn't get a chance to taste this pussy. You don't deserve something as sweet as this."

"Ebony is all the woman I need. You wish you could be half the woman she is."

That really pissed her off. Charlene grabbed one of the brass candleholders off the table and threw it at him. She then ran out of the door butt naked with her clothes in hand.

Chapter Twenty-One
Hold On

Maurice's head was spinning like he'd just gotten of the Tilt-A-Whirl at a county fair. He cherished his relationship with Ebony and didn't want to do anything to jeopardize it, but he knew he'd already gone too far.

How in the hell--Why in the hell did I let that happen? he thought.

Even though Charlene initiated the situation, Maurice felt guilty for letting it evolve to the point it did. He began questioning himself about love, wondering subconsciously if that's what he really wanted. Did he still want to be single and flexible? He wondered if that's why he let Charlene into his home in the first place.

He looked over at the phone and thought about calling Ebony, but he was afraid she'd sense that something was wrong. He didn't know how to tell her that her man and her best friend almost ended up doing the wild thang.

Maybe I shouldn't tell her anything, he thought. He quickly dismissed that notion because he was sure Charlene would delight in telling Ebony her version sooner or later.

He needed someone to talk to immediately. He tried calling Simon, but there was no answer. He figured that Simon was probably in the lounge with the rest of the guys as usual. Maurice decided to get dressed and pay Simon a visit.

"Simon will know what to do," he mumbled. Maurice took a quick shower, got dressed, hopped into his ride, and drove out to Atlantic Beach.

The traffic on his commute to the beach was a mess. Thanks to construction, the normal 15-minute drive took 45 minutes.

When Maurice arrived at Twilight, there was an ambulance parked at the front entrance with its lights flashing and rear doors open. Maurice noticed Carla standing next to the ambulance talking with one of the emergency medical technicians. He ran over to see what all the commotion was about.

"Hey, Carla, what's going on?" he asked nervously.

"Maurice, I'm glad you're here. It's Simon, he's--"

She was cut off when two EMTs burst through the doors pushing a stretcher. Maurice turned and saw Simon lying on the stretcher with an oxygen mask over his face and IV bags hanging. He immediately ran over to him.

Carla followed right behind him. They both began walking alongside Simon, who was lying unconscious.

Maurice turned to Carla. "What happened?" he asked.

"Simon had a stroke just moments ago. They're taking him to Baptist Medical Center."

Maurice turned and looked at the old man lying helplessly as the EMTs tried their best to hurry and get him in the ambulance.

"Hang in there, old-timer." Maurice's eyes watered. "It's going to be all right."

One of the EMTs turned towards Maurice. "Are you a relative?"

He immediately responded. "Yes, I'm his son."

"Well, you can ride with him in the back. Just keep talking to him," the EMT replied as they collapsed the wheels on the stretcher and slid it into the ambulance.

Maurice jumped into the back of the ambulance and sat next to Simon. He looked back at Carla, who by this time had tears rolling down her cheeks. All of the other guys had congregated outside as well. Each one of them was shedding tears.

Otis walked up to the ambulance. "Maurice, call me when you get to the hospital and let me know how he's doing. Take care of him."

"I'll call, I promise," Maurice replied.

The EMTs shut the ambulance doors and turned on the sirens. They sped to Baptist Medical Center, which was 10 minutes away. Maurice held onto Simon's hand as if his very life depended on it. One EMT was in the back of the ambulance with him, reading off vital signs into the radio.

"We're en route to the trauma unit with a stroke victim. He's an elderly male, age 67." The EMT began blurting out Simon's vital statistics.

Maurice couldn't interpret what the numbers meant, but by discerning the urgency in the man's voice, he knew that Simon was in serious trouble. "Don't you die on me, old man! Not now!" Maurice began to break down.

His mind was racing faster than the ambulance as it went through red lights and stop signs. Simon was one of the only people Maurice had left. He'd already lost his mother, and there's no way he wanted to lose Simon, the only father figure he had.

The ambulance roared down A1A. Maurice got more and more nervous as each second ticked by.

"Can this damn thing go any faster?" he yelled.

The EMT reached over and touched him on the shoulder. "Calm down, sir. It's going to be OK."

Maurice reacted in a hostile tone. "Don't you tell me to calm down! You need to get this piece of shit moving faster!"

The EMT turned away and continued doing his work. After a few moments of silence, Maurice realized he was way out of line for snapping at the guy who was just trying to do his job.

"Look, man, I'm sorry," Maurice apologized.

The EMT smiled. "Don't worry about it, sir. I know you're upset. Trust me, I see it all day long in this type of work. Apology accepted."

Maurice turned back to Simon. He could feel the old man's hands becoming colder as each minute passed. He put both of his hands on Simon's and bowed his head. He began to do something he hadn't done since the death of his mother: He prayed.

Lord, I know I haven't lived my life the way that You would've wanted it. All I'm asking is that You hear and answer this one prayer. Please let everything be OK with Simon. He's a good man. I know You have a purpose for him on this earth. Please don't take him. Not now, Lord, please. I beg You. In Jesus name, I pray. Amen.

Maurice became overwhelmed with emotion. He tried to hold back the flood of tears, but they spilled from his eyes. Just then he felt Simon begin to move his fingers. Maurice looked up and wiped his face. Simon's eyes were open and looking up toward the roof of the ambulance. Maurice's eyes widened.

"Simon, can you hear me?"

Simon turned and looked over at him, his lips curling into a faint smile.

Maurice began to laugh and sob simultaneously. Simon closed his eyes and fell unconscious again. Just then the ambulance came to an abrupt stop. They had finally arrived at the hospital. The ambulance doors flung open and the EMTs immediately went to work. Maurice stood by the stretcher holding Simon's hand the entire time.

They raced into the ER and down the hospital corridor until they came to an area that read, "Patients only beyond this point" above its swinging doors.

Maurice let go of Simon's hand but kept eye contact with him the whole time. He could've sworn the old man was smiling through his oxygen mask.

Maurice sat in the waiting room sipping on a cup of cappuccino from the vending machine. He couldn't believe that he was in a hospital again. He anxiously waited to hear from Simon's doctor. He finished his drink and began pacing back and forth frantically. He tried his best to think positive thoughts.

His cell phone rang, jarring him from his thoughts. He looked at the caller ID and saw that it was Ebony. He immediately answered the phone.

193

"Hello?"

"Hey, you. What's up? I've been trying to reach you all afternoon."

"I'm down at the hospital. Simon had a stroke."

"What? Is he OK?" she asked.

"I hope so, baby. I'm just waiting to hear back from the doctor right now."

"What hospital are you at?"

"I'm down at Baptist Medical."

"All right, I'm on my way."

"Love you, baby." Maurice never meant those words more.

"Love you too."

Ebony hung up the phone and grabbed her things. She knew how much Simon meant to Maurice. Just as she grabbed her purse the doorbell rang. When she opened the door, Charlene stood there.

"Hey, girl, you look like you're in a hurry."

"Yes, I am. Maurice's friend just had a stroke, and I'm on my way to meet him at the hospital."

Charlene gave Ebony a sour look. "Um." Charlene sighed with a bit of attitude.

What's all that about? Ebony thought.

"I'd love to hang around and chitchat, but I have to run." Ebony closed the door behind her.

"All right then, but make sure you give me a call later when you're finished. We *have* to talk."

Ebony nodded as she ran toward the parking lot. "Yeah, girl, I'll give you a call later!" she yelled over her shoulder.

Charlene stood in the walkway and watched as Ebony got into the car. "Yeah, we'll talk later, Ms. Thang."

Chapter Twenty-Two

Come Clean

When Ebony arrived at the hospital, she found Maurice staring out of the window, observing the view from the eighth floor. Simon lay in bed with tubes down his throat and an IV attached to his arm.

"Hey, you," Ebony whispered.

Maurice turned around. When their eyes met, they both felt a breeze of relief. Ebony ran over to him and hugged him tight. Maurice's eyes were puffy and red.

"Oh, baby." She lightly kissed his lips. "How's Simon doing?"

"He's stable right now, but I'm waiting to hear back from the doctor."

Ebony grabbed his hand and smiled. "He'll be just fine. Just keep thinking positively." Once again, Ebony knew how to brighten the darkest moments.

"I feel much better now that you're here," he whispered.

They both took a seat on the couch next to the window.

"Do you know what happened?" Ebony asked.

"They said he was playing cards with the guys when he all of a sudden passed out."

"I'm sure he'll be all right."

"Thanks so much for coming."

"I would've been here sooner, but I was tied up when I ran into Charlene."

Maurice felt his heart lodge in his throat when he heard that name. With everything that had just taken place with Simon, he'd forgotten about what had gone down earlier with Charlene. He knew Charlene hadn't said anything or Ebony would've already questioned him.

"Oh yeah? What did she want?"

"I'm not sure. She just said that she needed to talk to me about something."

Maurice wondered if Charlene would have the audacity to tell Ebony what went down. He knew she'd try to twist what had happened and make him look like the bad guy. Maurice figured he'd better be honest with Ebony and tell her what happened before she found out another way.

Maurice took a deep breath. "Sweetie, I need to talk to you."

Ebony noticed the pained look on his face. "Sure, what's up?"

"Let's take a walk."

They walked hand in hand out of Simon's room and went downstairs. They ventured outside to the patio and took a seat on a bench. Ebony turned to Maurice.

"So, what's up?"

"There's something I need to tell you."

"I'm listening?"

"It's about your friend Charlene." Ebony knitted her eyebrows. "What about her?"

Maurice felt his heart throbbing in his chest. "I was just chillaxin earlier, getting some rest and she showed up at my place."

Ebony was taken aback. "What did she want?"

Maurice looked away and closed his eyes. Knowing her past, he didn't want to see the hurt in Ebony's eyes when he told her.

"She wanted me."

"What?"

"She tried to make a move on me."

"You're joking, right?"

"I wish I were."

"So what happened? Did you do anything with her?" Ebony asked nervously, not knowing if she wanted to hear what had taken place.

"Well, no--not exactly."

"What the hell do you mean 'not exactly?' Either you did or you didn't." Ebony became enraged.

Maurice grabbed her by the hand, but she quickly jerked it away. That was the reaction he was afraid of.

"No, we didn't have sex, but--"

Ebony cut him off in mid-sentence. "But what, Maurice?"

Maurice didn't exactly know why, but he began telling her everything that had taken place. Ebony sat quietly and listened to what he had to say. After Maurice was finished, Ebony looked him directly in the eyes.

"I only have one question: If I hadn't called, would you have slept with Charlene?" she asked.

Maurice dropped his head. "You have to understand that everything happened so fast."

Ebony shook her head. "You didn't answer my question."

"I--I don't know."

"That's all I wanted to know." Ebony stood up and began walking toward the exit.

Maurice ran after her. "Where are you going?"

"I need some time to clear my head. It's already been a long day," she replied calmly.

"Well, at least let me walk you down to your car."

"No, it's OK. You should stay here with Simon. I'll be fine. I just need to get out for a while."

Maurice tried to hug her but she just turned away. Even though she didn't show it much, Maurice knew that she was hurting--and so was he.

Chapter Twenty-Three

Why Have I Lost You

One week had passed and Maurice hadn't heard anything from Ebony. He tried calling her at least three times a day, but she didn't return any of his calls. When he decided to stop by her studio, her assistant told him that she'd taken a vacation and was out of town.

That was the longest week of his life. He second-guessed himself time and time again, thinking that he should've just kept his mouth shut. He thought he'd picked the wrong time to be a boy scout.

The situation with Ebony was even affecting his music. During the band's last gig, Maurice had a few finger slips during his solo. In all of his years of playing the saxophone, he'd never made a mistake like that during a live performance. He had truly hit rock bottom.

Ebony and her cousin Monica sat in Aunt Shirley's living room, huddled around the coffee table having a session of girl talk. Monica convinced Ebony into taking a trip with her to Louisiana. Ebony was reluctant at first but later decided it was a good idea to go home and visit her people. Aunt Shirley seemed happier than Ebony remembered.

Desmond was the new man in Aunt Shirley's life, and they made a perfect couple. Their relationship had been going strong for a few months, and he'd even moved in with her.

Aunt Shirley walked into the living room with a tray of hot tea and freshly baked cookies, while Ebony and Monica went on and on about men.

"Man problems, huh?" Aunt Shirley asked as she handed a cup of tea to Ebony. "Looks like you've been crying for days, chile."

"That's seems to be the norm nowadays," Monica replied.

"Oh, what do you know about men?"

"Mama, I'm a grown woman. I know all I need to know."

"Well, you'd better lay off that fast food before you turn into an overgrown woman."

Ebony smiled.

"So, Ebony, tell me about this new man?"

"It's a long story, Aunt Shirley." Ebony picked up the mug of warm mint tea and took a sip.

"Girl, I've got nothing but time."

"She fell in love with this musician and now she's heartbroken," Monica blurted.

"I can tell my own story, Monica!"

"A musician, huh?" Aunt Shirley's interest piqued.

Ebony stared into her cup. "You're going to say the same thing. I should've known better than to date a musician."

"No, I wasn't going to say that. God works in mysterious ways, chile. I'm no one to judge."

"Everything was going so perfect. I should've known it was too good to be true. I just thought that maybe he was the one."

"So why did you guys break up?"

Ebony put the cup on the table and folded her arms. "Well, my prince charming and my best friend had a little encounter with each other."

"Ouch," Aunt Shirley said.

"Oh, Auntie, just when I start trusting a man again, this happens." Ebony began to weep.

"Trust me, girl, I know." Aunt Shirley reached over to soothe her niece. "I know the feeling."

Monica passed her cousin a tissue. Ebony softly dabbed at her tears.

Aunt Shirley continued, "Was this something they were doing behind your back?"

Ebony sniffled. "Not exactly. Charlene surprised him by showing up at his door dressed like the skank ho she is. I can't believe I trusted that bitch."

"So she was the one who initiated the whole situation?"

"Yeah, she seduced him, but Maurice should've known better. They didn't have sex, but they came close enough."

"Well, Ebony, you don't have to worry about that ho no mo'." Monica smiled.

Aunt Shirley looked at Monica out of the corner of her eye. "Don't tell me you've gotten into your cousin's business."

"Mama, what was I supposed to do?" Monica started. "After Ebony told me what happened, I went over to that heifer's apartment to beat her down."

Ebony began laughing. "You should've seen it. I've never seen Charlene run so fast."

"Now y'all know that's not the way to handle a situation like that," Aunt Shirley declared. "I raised you better than that, Monica. But I just have one question: Did you give her a good Bayou ass whippin'?

The women gave each other high fives. Ebony's laughs quickly turned into moans as she grabbed her stomach and excused herself. She rushed into the bathroom and began vomiting.

Monica leaned in to her mother. "Mama, she's been throwing up a lot. On our trip down here I had to keep pulling over so she could use the bathroom."

"Has she been acting funny lately?"

"Lots of mood swings. I think this situation with her boyfriend has her stressed out."

"Sounds like someone might have a little something in the oven. That explains that dream I had last night about fish."

Monica laughed at her mother's superstitious ways. Aunt Shirley was convinced that every time she dreamed about fish, someone she knew would end up pregnant.

A few minutes passed, and Ebony came walking back into the living room with a pale look on her face.

"Are you all right, chile?"

"I'll be OK, Aunt Shirley. Think I've picked up a virus."

Aunt Shirley raised an eyebrow. "You might've picked up a little more than that. When was your last period?"

"It was supposed to be last week. Why?"

Monica and her mother looked at each other and smiled. Ebony finally caught on to their insinuation.

"Nah, don't even go there. That's not even possible."

"Like I always say, chile, the Lord works in mysterious ways."

"But I can't have kids, remember? Bernard and I tried forever."

"Did you ever think the problem was with *him* and not *you*?" Aunt Shirley countered.

"Mama's got a point there, cuz," Monica said in between bites of a chocolate-chip cookie. "You told me yourself that y'all never had time to go to a fertility doctor to get checked out."

Ebony waved their comments away. "I love y'all, but both of you are trippin'. I'm not pregnant, and that's that."

A moment of silence engulfed the room. Aunt Shirley took Ebony's hands into hers. "I have just one question, baby. Do you love him?"

Ebony hesitated before answering, "Yes, I do."

"I'm a firm believer in second chances."

"Yeah, but--"

"We're all human, and everyone is capable of mistakes and bad judgment."

Ebony sat quietly and stared out the window.

"If this man is as good as you say his is, I'd give him another chance if I were you," Aunt Shirley lectured.

"I don't know, Auntie. That's why I waited a long time to get involved with someone again. I don't think this love thing is for me."

"Don't let one bad experience dictate your life, sweetheart. You can't have a future if you're stuck in the past."

Chapter Twenty-Four
I've Heard It All Before

Jamal and Chantel walked hand in hand along the boardwalk along Jacksonville Beach. It was a cool, breezy evening close to sunset. This was their first public outing. Their secret rendezvous usually took place at Jamal's luxurious home or at Chantel's house when her husband was gone for long periods of time. Both of them were becoming far too comfortable with their situation and lately began looking like a couple instead of sexual partners.

The boardwalk was busy with the usual beach traffic. Skaters and beach bums littered the walkway. Jamal and Chantel were on their way to the Blue Moon Café for happy hour. Chantel was looking stunningly sexy as usual, wearing a black miniskirt and a red halter, which revealed an ample amount of cleavage. She held onto Jamal's arm and admired the scenery.

"It's been a long time since I've walked near the beach," Chantel said wistfully.

"Sounds like you need to get out more often."

"That's the truth. My husband never takes me out. He's either too tired or away from home playing soldier."

"Why don't you just leave him?"

"Don't get me wrong. He's a good man, pays all the bills, and has good benefits, but I just need someone who can show me more attention and take care of my needs.

"He should be at home taking care of you. How could he let a woman as fine as you go without being satisfied." He grabbed Chantel's butt with the palm of his hand. "I'd be smacking this ass all day if I were him"

"I wish."

"You don't have to wish 'cause I'll make sure the job gets done."

Chantel licked her lips and smiled salaciously at him.

They walked onto the veranda at the Blue Moon Café and took a seat. The establishment wasn't one that was frequented by a lot of African-Americans, so Jamal figured it would be a good place to be incognito.

They ordered their drinks and a dish of hot wings for appetizers. Chantel excused herself to freshen up.

Jamal was busy checking out the ass of a beautiful blonde waitress when he felt a tap on his shoulder. He turned around and nearly jumped out of his skin when he looked into Nicole's eyes.

"Nicole! What are you doing here?"

"I decided to join some of the girls after work for drinks. I guess I should be asking what you're doing here, but I think I know," Nicole replied as she nodded towards Chantel, who was walking up to the table.

Jamal put his hand in his face and shook his head.

"Hello," Chantel said as she took her seat.

Nicole didn't even acknowledge that she was there.

"What do you want, Nicole?" Jamal continued.

"I can't believe you have the audacity to bring your little hoochie out in public."

"Excuse me?" Chantel rolled her neck in Nicole's direction.

"Oh, you heard me." Nicole didn't back down.

Chantel pushed her chair back from her table and was about to stand up.

Jamal reached over and grabbed her by the arm. "Chill out, Chantel."

"You know what," Nicole began, "I'm not even going to trip. You're not even worth it."

"There's nothing to trip about. You know what's up with you and me--not a goddamn thing!"

Nicole's eyes became slits. She wanted desperately to go upside his head with a chair. "You're right, Jamal. But remember, what goes around comes around."

She turned around and walked back over to the table where her friends were sitting. All of them were looking at Jamal like a pack of hungry jackals.

"Who was that crazy bitch?" Chantel asked.

"My old girlfriend."

"She was about two seconds from getting her ass whipped."

"Don't even sweat it. She's just salty 'cause I gave her the boot."

Jamal and Chantel quickly finished their drinks, and Jamal signaled the waitress for the check. After paying the bill, they made a hasty exit from the Blue Moon Café. Jamal didn't even look in the direction of Nicole and her friends, but he could feel their eyes looking his way. Chantel held onto Jamal's arm and walked with a smile. Jamal breathed a sigh once they were back on the boardwalk and heading for the parking lot.

"Looks like you're going to have problems when you get home," Chantel stated. "That's what you get for laying that good dick on all of these weak-minded little girls."

"I can't help it if they all want of piece of Mandingo," Jamal boasted.

Jamal pressed the unlock button on his remote and opened the door for Chantel. Just as he walked around to the driver's side, he noticed a piece of paper taped to the door handle. As he reached for the note, the car parked behind him turned on its bright lights. Jamal used his hand to shield his eyes. A black Maxima backed up and screeched off into traffic.

Jamal grabbed the piece of paper and unfolded it. The note was in bold letters written with a marker:

YOU'LL GET WHAT YOU DESERVE, MOTHERFUCKER!

Jamal was furious. He balled up the note and threw it on the ground.

"What was that about?" Chantel inquired.

"I ought to go back in there and smack that bitch."

"What are you talking about?"

"That's the fourth time she's left me a note like that."

"Who?"

"Nicole. She's been leaving me threatening messages and doing shit to my car."

"Sounds like you've got a psycho on your hands."

"I know she's the one behind it."

"Don't worry about it, baby. Let's just head back to your place." Chantel reached over and grabbed his crotch. "I have a little something that'll make you forget about that tramp."

"Yeah, fuck that ho. I'll get her ass later." Jamal backed out of the parking space and headed to his place for a long night of bumping and grinding.

Chapter Twenty-Five

It's Over Now

The headboard banged loudly against the wall of Jamal's bedroom, while the bed beneath them squeaked for relief. Chantel sat on top, riding him like a champion bull rider. Her hands gripped the edge of the mattress as she pulled for leverage. Her braids swung violently.

"What's my name?" Jamal demanded.

"Jamal!" she screamed.

He thrust harder and deeper as Chantel bounced up and down on his jimmy.

"Say it louder!" he demanded.

"Jamal! Jamal!"

After 30 minutes of wild humping, Chantel grew quiet. Her body began to quiver, and her breathing increased. Within seconds her body started to shake. He knew she was close to climax so he began to rotate his hips in a circular motion.

"Yeah, baby! Keep doing that!" she yelled.

Within seconds Chantel let out a loud gasp. She exploded in an intense orgasm that sent a sensual shockwave throughout the room.

Not wanting to be outdone, Jamal rolled her over and positioned her doggy-style. He grabbed a pillow and put under her stomach. He began thrusting into her anew.

"Whose pussy is it?" Jamal forcefully pulled her braids.

Chantel was moaning and cooing all in one breath. "It's yours, baby! It's...all...yours!"

"That's right! Your husband wishes he could satisfy you like this!" Jamal continued to boast. He drew back his hand and slapped her on the ass.

Chantel winced. "Take it easy, baby. Not too hard."

Jamal was in a freaky frenzy, increasing the pace of his strokes. "You know you like that, don't you?"

"I do, baby, I do!" Chantel screamed. "Fuck me! Fuck me!"

They continued their wild banging for the next hour. Chantel knew she'd be sore in the morning, but she didn't care. After their sexual session they lay in bed resting up for another round. Chantel sat up to smoke a cigarette, and they heard the doorbell ring.

"Who the hell is that this late at night?" Jamal griped.

"Probably another one of your *associates*," Chantel smirked.

Jamal wondered if it was Nicole. *After the scene at the restaurant and the note on his car that night, he knew that she was capable of anything. But as crazy as she was she knew better than to show up at his place without calling first.*

The person began knocking very hard.

"Wait a minute!" Jamal yelled from the bathroom and went to investigate. He put on his robe. The knock at the door became louder and constant.

"Quit knocking on the door like the damn police," he shouted. Jamal opened the door quickly. He was so angry that he didn't even look through his peephole to see who was on the other side.

"What the fuck do you want?" he asked as he swung the door open. To his surprise, no one was there. Jamal stepped onto his front step and noticed the same black Maxima that blinded him earlier in the parking lot parked right in front of his house. He balled up his fist and grunted. Nicole drove a Honda Accord, but he figured she borrowed the car from one of her friends to do her dirty work. He'd had enough of this little cat-and-mouse stalking game. He figured he'd get dressed and get ready to whip some ass.

"I'm going to get this bitch," he mumbled.

Just as Jamal turned to go back into the house to get his pants and pistol, he felt a sharp pain in the back of his neck. Everything went black.

When Jamal woke up, he found himself strapped to one of his dining room chairs. His robe was no longer wrapped around him; he sat nude tied to the chair. He could hear the sound of someone crying coming from his bedroom. He remembered Chantel.

Jamal wanted to scream, but the duct tape around his mouth prevented him from uttering a single sound. It was wrapped so tightly that it hurt to even move his head. His hands were roped behind his back, and his ankles were attached to the legs of the chair. The rope was beginning to burn his wrists as he squirmed and struggled to get loose.

Suddenly Chantel stumbled in from the bedroom. She was limping, and her face was bloody. A huge man stood behind her with a gun pointed to the back of her head. They both walked toward Jamal. Chantel was crying and breathing heavily. Jamal could tell by the look in her eyes that she feared for her life. Her bottom lip trembled uncontrollably.

"I'm sorry! I'm so sorry!" Chantel cried.

"Shut the hell up, cunt!" the man yelled. He pushed her in the back, causing her to fall to the floor next to where Jamal was sitting.

The large man towered over them with a delirious look on his face. Jamal thought he was being robbed. He and the intruder locked eyes for a moment, staring each other down. For some reason, the man's face looked really familiar, but Jamal couldn't remember where he'd seen him.

"Well, well, well," the man said, "I've been waiting for this moment for a long time. I've been watching you for a while now." He grinned deviously. "You're the infamous Jamal Grover, the man with the golden voice who goes around fucking with people's lives."

Jamal tensed up and balled his fist, wanting badly to kick this guy's ass. But he was in no position to be brave and prideful. The man bent down in front of Jamal, breath reeking of alcohol. He looked down between Jamal's legs.

"Looks like your balls are shaking, nigga." He reached into his side pocket and pulled out a sharp combat knife. "Maybe I should cut them off first--to see how high you can really sing." The man laughed uncontrollably.

He continued his taunting speech. "Oh, I'm sorry, I didn't formally introduce myself. My name is Daryl, Chantel's soon-to-be ex-husband." He smiled and looked at Chantel.

Jamal finally recognized him. He remembered seeing his pictures on Chantel's dresser at her place.

The black Maxima, the letters. This is the son of a bitch, Jamal thought.

"Daryl, please! What about the kids?" Chantel pleaded with huge tears of fear rolling down her cheeks.

Daryl walked over to her and kicked her in the abdomen. Chantel cried out and grabbed her stomach.

"Shut the fuck up, bitch!" he shouted. "You wasn't thinking about the kids when you were fucking this motherfucker, were you?"

Jamal was helpless. If only he could get his hands untied, he'd at least be able to put up a fight. There was no way he wanted to go out like a sissy tied to a chair. But at this point, he was terrified. If he could beg for his life, he would.

Daryl paced back and forth with the 9mm Glock in his hand. He walked over to a gym bag he'd placed next to the couch and pulled out a videotape.

"Y'all have to see this shit right here!" he announced, laughing hysterically. "This is some good stuff!"

Daryl walked over to the entertainment center and put the tape in the VCR. He pressed play and walked back over to the bag. He pulled out a pint of Jack Daniels and took a big swig. Jamal and Chantel both trembled with fear.

The television came on. The tape was in black and white like some type of security video. Chantel immediately recognized the view of her own bedroom. On the tape were she and Jamal, caught in the act of sexing each other in her bed in every way possible. Chantel gasped for air, her breath literally taken away from her.

"See what I'm talking bout?" Daryl belched and wiped his sweaty face with the back of his hand. "I've got my own personal porno of my wife fucking around while I'm busting my ass working hard for my family!"

He turned to Jamal. "Damn, dog, I gotta give it to you. You were really tearing that ass up!"

"I'm sorry, Daryl!" Chantel pleaded. "Please let me explain."

Daryl turned to Chantel. He pointed his military issue pistol directly at her.

"Explain what, bitch?" he screamed. "There's nothing to explain. Seems to me like you and your fuck friend were having a good time at my expense."

"It wasn't like that, Daryl. I--"

"Didn't I tell you to shut the hell up?" he interrupted. "If I hear another word, I promise I'll make it a slow death."

Jamal's heart was beating faster than a black man running from the L.A.P.D. All he could think about was what Maurice always told him about messing with married women. His mind raced like Carl Lewis as he tried to think of ways to get out of this mess. Jamal began to moan so he could get Daryl's attention.

"Ummm!" he moaned, sounding like a mummy. "Ummm!"

Daryl walked over to Jamal and bent down in front of him. "Well, looks like the little bitch wants to talk." He pulled the combat knife from his waistband. "I'm going to cut this tape off, but if you try to yell, I'll gut your ass like a salmon."

Jamal nodded in agreement. Daryl cut the duct tape from Jamal's mouth. He took a deep gasp for air.

"So, what does the little bitch have to say?" Daryl asked.

Jamal's voice trembled. "Look, bro, I'm sorry for all the confusion. But I--"

"Motherfucker, I don't even want to hear it!" Daryl interrupted.

Jamal now found himself staring down the barrel of the gun. Memories of his life flashed in front of his face in slow motion. He thought for sure he was done.

"I'm trained in over a thousand ways to take a life. Now which one should I use to take yours?"

Jamal began sobbing like a kid knowing he was about to get a whipping by his father. "I'm sorry, man! Don't do this!" Jamal pleaded.

Daryl got right in Jamal's face. He began to sniff his skin. "You know what? I smell nothing but bitch. Is that what you are? A little punk-ass bitch?"

At this point Jamal didn't care about pride. He just wanted to live. He was now sobbing uncontrollably.

"Don't!" Chantel cried.

Daryl turned to his wife. "Oh, so now you're standing up for your man, huh?"

Daryl walked over to Chantel and lifted the 9mm to the side of her head. The room filled with silence as she closed her eyes. Daryl fired a single shot into the side of her head. Jamal's heart stopped momentarily as he watched Chantel's lifeless body fall to the floor. He was frozen with fear and shock. Somehow he managed to scream.

219

"No!" he yelled. "You son of a bitch!"

Jamal tried his best to move around and break free from the rope. He was screaming and jerking frantically. Daryl lifted the gun, pointed it right between Jamal's eyes, and squeezed the trigger.

Chapter Twenty-Six
Is This The End?

If I hadn't called, would you have slept with Charlene?

Maurice was tormented with this question since he had last seen Ebony. It was a question that he honestly couldn't answer. Maybe it was fate that Ebony called to rescue him--or maybe it was chance? Either way, he was now alone and missing Ebony more than ever. He looked at a picture of them together and his heart broke a little more.

He gathered his keys to get out of his house to get some fresh air. As he was about to step out the door, the phone rang. He rushed to get it before the voicemail picked up.

"Hello?" he said, hoping to hear Ebony's voice.

"Hey, Maurice. How's it going?" It was Nicole. It had been a long time since she'd called him, so he knew something was up.

"Not much, Nicole. What's up?"

There was a slight pause and then Nicole asked, "Is Jamal there with you?"

"No, I haven't seen him. Did you try to reach him on his cell?"

"I tried, but I keep getting his voicemail. We had another argument last night, and I just have a bad feeling."

Maurice could tell by the sound of her voice that she had been crying. "A bad feeling about what? You guys have been through this a thousand times."

"I don't know what it is, Mo, but something just doesn't feel right. I hate it when I feel like this because something bad always happens."

Maurice figured Jamal was probably out with some fine young thang that he seduced. "Did you stop by his house?"

"That's why I'm calling. I don't want to go over there and get my feelings hurt. Knowing him, he's probably laid up with some hoochie."

You're probably right about that, Maurice thought.

"All right, sis, I'll try to track him down if it'll make you feel better."

"Thanks, Maurice. Why can't Jamal just be a good man like you?"

"Trust me, I'm no angel. I've had my days of dirty deeds."

"Well, the important thing you just said is that you *had* those days. Jamal still wants to live in those days and not grow up."

"I commend you for hanging in there and sticking by his side. Hopefully one of these days he'll have some sense knocked into that dome of his."

"I hope so. Thanks for this, Maurice. I really needed someone to talk to. Just give me a call when you see him. I'm really worried."

"You can put your mind at ease. Detective Maurice is on the case," he joked.

"All right then, Mo. I'll talk to you later."

"Don't worry, I'll find him."

Maurice realized that he hadn't heard from Jamal all day, which was unusual. He picked up his cell and called him. The phone rang and rang, but no answer. The voicemail picked up, and Maurice left a message.

"Yo. player, give me a holler when you get this message. I haven't heard from you in a minute. Hit me back. One love."

Nicole's bad feeling now started to affect Maurice. He knew it was odd for his boy to be out of touch for so long. Maurice ran out to his roadster and burned off toward Jamal's place.

When Maurice arrived at Jamal's place, he noticed all the lights were on inside. He pulled up behind the car that was parked in Jamal's driveway.

"Looks like the Trojan has company," he mumbled.

He figured Jamal was probably knocking the bottom out of some fine female.

As Maurice walked towards the door, he glanced into the open passenger window and saw empty alcohol bottles and a camouflage jacket across the front seat. A tingling feeling of nervousness began to consume him, and his adrenaline started to kick in.

Maurice quickly turned around and ran back to his car. Living in a big city taught him one thing: to always be prepared because you could be jacked at anytime. He reached under the driver's seat and pulled out a lockbox. Inside was his gun. He inserted the clip and walked back toward the house. He thought about calling the police, but he forgot his cell phone at the house.

"Damn, can't believe I left my damn phone," he griped.

Maurice approached the house from the side. He tried to peek in the window, but he could only see the glow of the lights. The air was filled with an eerie silence. No barking dogs, no cars passing, no crickets chirping--just silence.

He decided to head around back to see if the back door was open. He slowly crept around to the rear of the house. When he got to the back door he was surprised to find it open. Maurice turned the doorknob and slowly opened the door. He walked in with his gun raised. He'd seen police do it a million times on television, so he just mimicked their actions.

He moved carefully through the back of the kitchen, walking from heel to toe, trying not to make a sound. He could hear sounds coming from the television in the living room. He slowly ventured into the living room with his gun still out in front of him. Just as he entered the living room, his nostrils filled with the stench of death.

Maurice vomited at the sight before him. Next to the television was a man lying facedown on the floor. His head was blown wide open, and brain matter was everywhere.

When Maurice turned around, he almost passed out when he saw his best friend strapped to a chair with rope. Jamal's lifeless eyes were open and a small bloody hole sat right between them. Maurice's knees began to weaken as he walked over to Jamal. Chantel's body was lying on the floor next to Jamal's. The side of her head was blown open.

Maurice started sobbing.

Chapter Twenty-Seven
It's So Hard To Say Goodbye To Yesterday

The old cathedral was filled to capacity. Members of the press were camped outside, waiting like vultures hovering over a fresh kill. Jamal's funeral had drawn a lot of attention. Fans lined up outside the church to pay their final respects. Everyone in the pews was dressed in black.

The MoJazz band members sat on the front pew. They were all pallbearers. Maurice and Nicole sat next to Jamal's mother and sister. They'd made the grueling trip from Miami.

Mrs. Grover sat straight faced throughout the entire service, not once showing the least bit of emotion. She knew it would only be a matter of time before something like this happened. She saw it as being a generational curse. Her husband, Jamal's father, died the exact same way. She tried to warn him that messing around would catch up to him one day, but he never listened.

It was a closed-casket service. On top of the pearl casket were flowers and pictures of Jamal at different stages of his life. There was even one when he was three years old, holding a microphone. The last picture was of him and Maurice onstage doing what they both enjoyed.

Friends and family gave emotional speeches to the congregation. Maurice was the last to speak. As he approached the podium he tried his best to keep his composure. He wished that Ebony were there with him. He knew that he'd have the strength if he could only look into those beautiful eyes and see her exquisite smile once again. But she wasn't there, and his life had to go on.

"I don't know where to start," Maurice began to speak. "I have so many things to say *to* Jamal Grover. He was much more than my best friend. He was my brother. So, instead of giving a speech, I want to express myself in the only way I know how."

Chauncey walked up to the podium and handed Maurice his soprano saxophone.

"I wrote a musical piece that I would like to dedicate to my best friend and to someone that made me realize what life and love are all about. It's entitled 'Saxual Feelings.'"

Maurice began to blow into the instrument and a soothing hush filled the church. The blissful sounds of the sax echoed throughout the cathedral. It was a very emotional and spiritual experience.

Maurice put his all into the piece as tears began streaming down his face. He pictured everything that he and Jamal had gone through over the years. When he finished the tune, there wasn't a dry eye in the place. Everyone was consumed by the emotion that Maurice rendered through his brass horn.

Just as Maurice completed his piece, he looked up at the congregation. They all stood to their feet and applauded. Maurice noticed a woman standing at the entrance of the church. She was dressed in a black business suit with a matching hat. As the congregation continued to applaud, the woman made her way down the center aisle. Maurice's heart literally skipped a beat when he looked into Ebony's eyes.

Maurice stepped down from the podium and met Ebony at the front pew. They both hugged and embraced each other while the congregation continued to applaud.

Epilogue
Now That We've Found Love

It was a warm, sunny Saturday afternoon. Not one cloud interrupted the clear blue sky above. Maurice was on his way to meet with Ebony and Simon for the groundbreaking ceremony. Jamal left him a sizeable amount of money in his will, so Maurice decided to give back and finally realize his dream of building the creative arts and sports center for the youth of Jacksonville.

Maurice smiled to himself as he listened to the radio while cruising along A1A highway. The DJ had just introduced the new hit song that everyone was talking about: "Saxual Feelings" by MoJazz.

He knew "Saxual Feelings" was something special when he wrote it. During the dreadful time right after he'd lost Jamal, the only comfort he had was his saxophone. He played and played until his lungs could blow no more. The song was his expression of emotions bottled up inside.

A few weeks after writing the music, he added soul-shaking lyrics that put the icing on the cake. Though Jamal could never be replaced, Devon laid the vocals and did his fallen brother proud. The end product captured the soul and wouldn't let go until you felt its vibe.

MoJazz was now firmly on its way. Its grassroots success caused a bidding war among major record labels. The group ended up accepting a deal with Platinum Music Group based out of Atlanta. The two-album deal was the beginning of a new era for MoJazz. Tracks Jamal had laid would be released posthumously. His lifelong dream would be realized in death.

It was a little after two o'clock when Maurice pulled up to the grassy field. A stage was set up in the center with chairs in front of it and brightly colored balloons everywhere. Kids were running around playing games and having fun. A few reporters gathered near the podium and were conducting interviews with dignitaries and other community guests.

A group of young boys were playing football and noticed Maurice's arrival. Once they saw him, they came running from every direction. Anita's son, Malik, led the pack. As Maurice got out of his car, the kids jumped all over him.

"Uncle Mo! Uncle Mo!" Malik yelled as he ran up to Maurice and tried to tackle him.

"Slow down, dynamite!" Maurice reached down to scoop Malik up in a big bear hug.

"Come on, let's play some football, Unc!"

All of the other children joined in with Malik and pleaded for Maurice to join them in playing catch.

"I'd love to, kids, but let me get through this ceremony first. Then I'll show y'all young bucks how to play a real man's game."

Ebony snuck up behind Maurice and hugged him around the waist. "Just make sure this so-called real man doesn't get hurt. I want to enjoy this time with my husband without us going to the emergency room." She laughed.

Maurice turned and smiled as he looked into her beautiful brown eyes. "Hey, sweetie," he replied, and they kissed briefly.

Malik frowned. "Ew, y'all nasty."

"Boy, mind your business and get ready to catch this pass!" Maurice grabbed the ball out of Malik's grasp.

Malik got in a runner's stance while another one of the little boys defended him.

"Set, hut one, hut two, hike!"

Malik took off running as fast as he could, straight down the middle of the field. Maurice was amazed at just how fast Malik could run. "Keep going!" Maurice yelled.

Malik was running in full stride when Maurice released the ball. He outran his defender by at least 10 yards, which would be considered burning an opponent in a real game. He looked over his shoulder as he tried to position himself to catch the ball. He was open all by himself when the ball popped in and out of his hands. Some of the kids laughed and teased him.

Malik picked up the ball and came back to Maurice with his head hung low. "Sorry, Uncle Mo."

"Don't worry bout that, Malik. We'll work on catching the football." Maurice patted him on the back. He could tell the youngster was disappointed. But Maurice encouraged him and told him that he'd get better with practice.

Ebony observed the interaction between the two. "You're going to make a good father," she announced.

Maurice walked over to Ebony and started talking to her rotund stomach.

"You hear that, little Mo? I can't wait for you to get here so we can start training you to play running back!"

Ebony playfully punched Maurice on the shoulder. "Now don't you start with that. You insisted that you didn't want to know the sex."

"Oh, believe me, I know. You're gonna surprise me with a boy."

"I told you to keep your job as a musician because you suck as a psychic." Ebony laughed.

"Well, we'll just see in a couple days now, won't we?"

"With all the excitement, let's hope I don't go into labor today."

Maurice was ecstatic at the blessing of becoming a father. When Ebony had told him that she was pregnant he jumped at the chance to do the right thing. He didn't want to lose the love of his life--and his child.

Carmen popped up with a cute bundle of joy at their wedding, screaming that Maurice was the father. She briefly caused a scene at the wedding reception, but Monica took care of that problem really quickly.

A few weeks after that dramatic incident, Maurice took a paternity test. The test was conclusive--he was not the father. Carmen was no longer an issue in his life.

Maurice and Ebony walked over to the tent to the left of the stage, where all of the grown folks were hanging out. Simon and the rest of the older guys were decked out in three-piece suits, looking debonair with an old-school flare. Even away from the nursing home, they were still doing what they did best: playing spades and talking shit about women.

"What's up, old-timers?" Maurice asked as he and Ebony took a seat at a nearby table.

"Just having a good time, MoJazz," Simon replied.

"Did you pick up that pack of Kools from the store?" asked Otis.

"Come on, Otis. I told you I'm not gonna buy you no more cigarettes. You might want to kill yourself, but I'm not going to help."

"Looky here, what I tell you 'bout talking to me like that, youngster? I'm not a killer, but don't push me," Otis snapped.

"There he goes again. Talking more trash," Clyde joined in.

"All right, don't get started. Today's a good day, and no one wants to hear you geezers arguing," Simon interrupted.

Otis gave his usual evil-eye routine while peering over the top of his glasses, but his expression softened when Carla walked up arm in arm with a handsome man. "Aw, there she is. Congratulations, baby girl. Twilight ain't gonna be the same without you."

"Thank you, fellas. I'm gonna miss y'all, but my baby is moving and so am I." Carla blushed, and her beau hugged her tighter. Maurice recognized him as the EMT who helped Simon when he fell ill.

"You just be sure to write, you hear?" Simon said, smiling at her happiness.

Simon turned his attention to Maurice. "I'm proud of what you're doing here for the kids, MoJazz."

"Well, I learned from the best. I figure these kids need a place let off all that steam and creative energy."

Simon gave Maurice the look of a proud father. "Thanks, MoJazz. You don't know how much that means to me."

Ebony walked over to Simon and gave him a kiss on the cheek. "You're the best, Simon."

"Boy, you sure do have yourself a fine woman here." Simon hugged Ebony tight.

"I know that's right," Maurice replied.

"Y'all ought to quit," Ebony teased.

"Well, I guess you better get started with the ceremony. The press has been waiting long enough. You know us black folks can never start an event on time," Simon joked.

Everyone left the tent and gathered around the stage. Next to the podium stood an object covered with a large white sheet. Ebony was in full swing with her camera, doing what she loved most. Plenty of flashbulbs flickered when Maurice stepped up to the podium and grabbed the microphone. A silence fell over the crowd as Maurice was about to speak.

"Testing, testing." He smiled while tapping the microphone. "First of all, I'd like to say thank everyone for coming out and being a part of this important day in the life of our community. This day is truly history in the making. Today we're taking another step in advancing the dreams of our youth.

"African-Americans make up only a small portion of our nation's population, but we make up an enormous portion of the prison population. We're losing our young people, y'all. Today I'd like to challenge everyone to do something, especially the black men! I'm by no means a preacher or an activist, but I do know that just one person can make a difference.

"It doesn't take riches to change a person's life. Something as simple as spending more time with the youth can have an enormous influence on their lives. Let's be there for our kids."

The crowd shook with applause.

"That's why I'd like to dedicate this center and program to the person who has had a great influence on my life. Even when I was bullheaded and didn't want to listen, he was still there to give me advice and guidance. We need more people like him today, someone from the old guard who exemplifies what it means to be a real man. He provides something far more than just knowledge. He provides wisdom. And for that I'm eternally grateful."

Maurice walked over and removed the sheet from the object next to the podium. It revealed a bronze engraved plaque that included the mission statement of the center. The four-foot plaque was designed in the shape of a piano with the name of the center engraved at the top.

"It's with great pride and honor that I present to you the future site of the Simon Winters Center for Youth! Simon, this is for you!"

The crowd erupted into applause once again as everyone turned to Simon and applauded him. The old man was overcome with emotion and began to cry. Maurice walked over and embraced him as he sat in his wheelchair.

At that moment, Maurice felt as if his mother was smiling down on him. Finally he'd grown up and was moving in the direction that she would have approved of. For the first time, every part of his life played in perfect harmony.

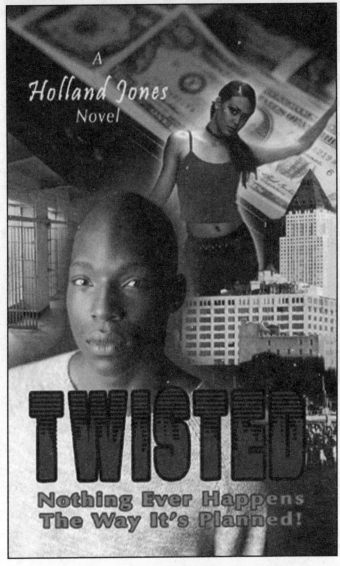

" T W I S T E D "
DESCRIPTION

Nadine, a sultry, ghetto-fine conniving gold-digger, will do whatever it takes to make sure that she is financially set for life -- even at the cost of breaking-up a family.

When Wayne, Nadine's man since high-school, is sentenced to two years in prison for a crime he did not commit, he's betrayed by the two people he trusted the most—his woman (Nadine) and his cousin (Bobo).

Asia, a curvaceous diva and designer-clothing boutique owner with a wilder-side sexual-preference becomes an unlikely confidant to her best-friend Nadine's man (Wayne) during his incarceration.

Meanwhile Bobo, one of VA's most notorious and most successful Street-Entreprenuers, manages to hustle his way into staring down a possible life sentence.

Now that the roles are reversed, it's Bobo who's now facing some serious prision time, as Nadine tries to do whatever it takes to keep her hands on the secret stash of cash hidden in a suitcase that Bobo left behind.

Money, greed and sex always have as a way of gettin' things *Twisted!*

"Daaaaayummmmmm! Holland Jones brings it! A hood-licious story that combines deceit, murder, freaky sex and mysterious-twists! You gotta get this one!"

-- Winston Chapman, Best-Selling Author of *Caught Up!* and *Wild Thangz*

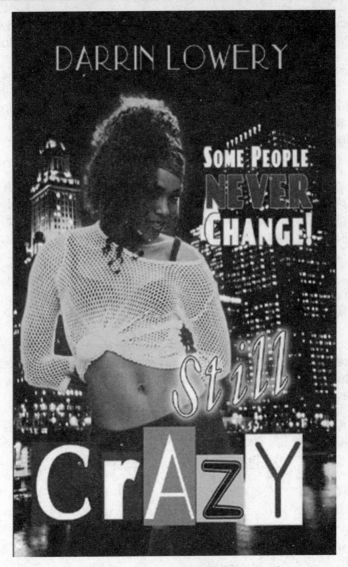

"STILL CRAZY"
DESCRIPTION

Kevin Allen, a rich, handsome author and self-reformed 'Mack', is now suffering from writer's block.

Desperately in need of a great story in order to renegotiate with his publisher to maintain his extravagant life-style, Kevin decides to go back to his hometown of Chicago for inspiration. While in Chi-town, he gets reacquainted with an ex-love (Yolanda) that he'd last seen during their stormy relationship that violently came to an end.

Unexpectedly, Yolanda appears at a book-event where Kevin is the star-attraction, looking every bit as stunningly beautiful as the picture he's had frozen in his head for years. She still has the looks of music video model and almost makes him forget as to the reason he'd ever broken off their relationship.

It's no secret, Yolanda had always been the jealous type. And, Kevin's explanation to his boyz, defending his decision for kicking a woman that fine to the curb was, "She's Crazy!".

The combination of Kevin's vulnerable state in his career, along with the tantalizing opportunity to hit *that* again, causes Kevin to contemplate renewing his expired Players-Card, one last time. What harm could one night of passion create?

Clouding his judgment even more is that Kevin feels like hooking-up with Yolanda might just be the rekindling needed to ignite the fire for his creativity in his writing career. But, there are just two problems. Kevin is married! ....And, Yolanda is *Still Crazy!*

"Darrin Lowery deliciously serves up…..Scandal & Sexy-Drama like no other! *STILL CRAZY* has all the goods readers are looking for!"

-- *Brenda Hampton, Author of "Slick"*

" C R U N K "
DESCRIPTION

Imagine a Thug-World divided by the Mason-Dixon Line........

After the brutal murder of four NYC ganstas in Charlotte, the climate is set for an all-out Thug Civil War – North pitted against South!

Rah-Rah, leader of NYC's underworld and KoKo, head of one of the Durty South's most ferocious Crunk-crews are on a collision course to destruction. While Rah-Rah tries to rally his northern Thugdom (Philly, NJ & NY), KoKo attempts to saddle-up heads of the southern Hoodville (Atlanta, South Carolina & Charlotte).

Kendra and Janeen, a southern sister-duo of self-proclaimed baddest b*****'s, conduct a make-shift Thug Academy to prepare KoKo's VA-bred cousin (Shine) to infiltrate NYC's underground, as a secret weapon to the impending battle.

The US Government, well-aware of the upcoming war, takes a backseat role, not totally against the idea that a war of this magnitude might actual do what the Government has been unable to do with thousands of life sentences -- Rid society completely of the dangerous element associated with the Underground-World.

Suspensfully-Sexy, Erotically-Ghetto and Mysteriously-Raw. CRUNK will leave you saying, Hmmmm?

"Get Ready For A Wild & Sexy Ride! Twists & Turns Are Abundant! An Instant Urban Classic Thriller! Tariq, Rudd & Jones Are Definitely Some BAD BOYZ! Errr'body Gettin' CRUNK!"

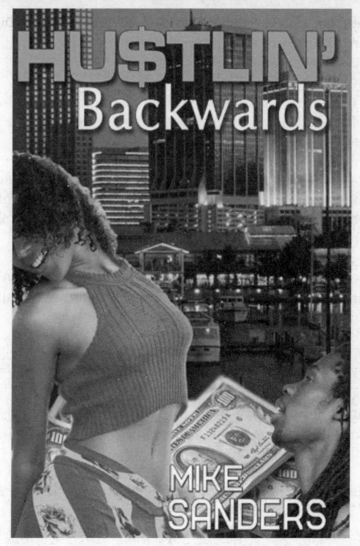

"Hustlin' Backwards"
DESCRIPTION

Capone and his life-long road dawgz, June and Vonzell are out for just one thing.... To get rich!....By any means necessary!

As these three partners in crime rise up the ranks from Project-Kids to Street-Dons, their sworn code of "Death Before Dishonor" gets tested by the Feds.

Though Capone's simple pursuit of forward progression as a Hustler gains him an enviable lifestyle of Fame, Fortune and all the women his libido can handle – It also comes with a price.

No matter the location – Miami, Charlotte, Connecticut or Puerto Rico – There's simply no rest for the wicked!

WARNING: HUSTLIN' BACKWARDS is not the typical street-novel. A Unique Plot, Complex Characters mixed with a Mega-dose of Sensuality makes this story enjoyable by all sorts of readers! A true Hustler himself, Mike Sanders knows the game, inside and out!

"Fast-Paced and Action-Packed! Hustlin' Backwards HAS IT ALL -- Sex, Money, Manipulation and Murder! Mike Sanders is one of the most talented and prolific urban authors of this era!"

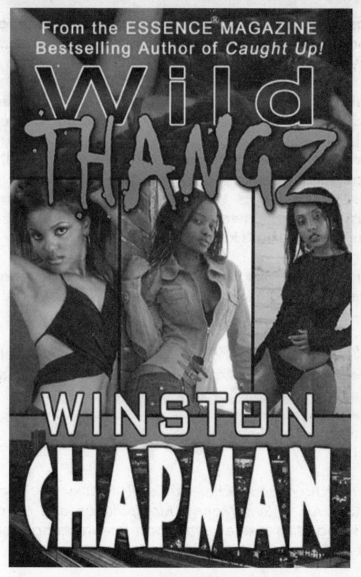

"Wild Thangz"
DESCRIPTION

Jazmyn, Trina and Brea are young & fine with bangin'
bodies and are in the midst of their sexual peak.

As they explore different paths towards their own
individual goals in life, these drama-magnets learn
invaluable lessons from experience and each other.

Lust, temptation and greed test the limits of their
friendship bond.

It is what they have in common that leads the trio
repeatedly into all kinds of trouble.

Wild Parties, Wild Situations & Wild Nights are always
present for these Wild Thangz!

*"Wild Thangz is HOT! Winstson Chapman shonuff
brings the HEAT!"* -- Mysterious Luva, Essence
Magazine Best-Selling Author of "Sex A Baller"

"Sex A Baller"
DESCRIPTION

Mysterious Luva has sexed them all! Ball players, CEO's, Music Stars -- You name the baller, she's had them. And more importantly, she's made them all pay......

Sex A Baller is a poignant mix of a sexy tale of how Mysterious Luva has become one of the World's Best Baller Catchers and an Instructional Guide for the wanna-be Baller Catcher!

No details or secrets are spared, as she delivers her personal story along with the winning tips & secrets for daring women interested in catching a baller!

PLUS, A SPECIAL BONUS SECTION INCLUDED!

Baller Catching 101

- Top-20 Baller SEX POSITIONS (Photos!)
- Where To FIND A Baller
- Which Ballers Have The BIGGEST Penis
- SEDUCING A Baller
- Making A Baller Fall In Love
- Getting MONEY From A Baller
- What Kind Of SEX A Baller Likes
- The EASIEST Type of Baller To Catch
- Turning A Baller Out In Bed
- GAMES To Play On A Baller
- Getting Your Rent Paid & A Free Car
- Learn All The SECRETS!

BY THE END OF THIS BOOK, YOU'LL HAVE YOUR CERTIFIED BALLER-CATCHER'S DEGREE!

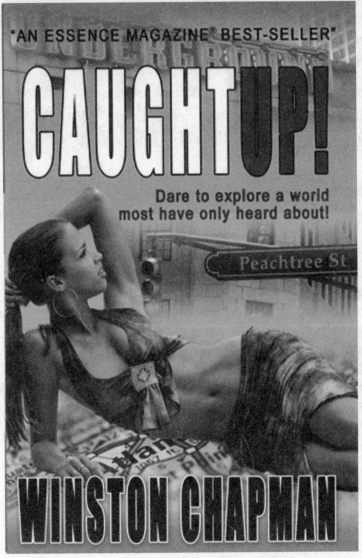

"CAUGHT UP!"
DESCRIPTION

When Raven Klein, a bi-racial woman from Iowa moves to Atlanta in hopes of finding a life she's secretly dreamed about, she finds more than she ever imagined.

Quickly lured and lost in a world of sex, money, power-struggles, betrayal & deceit, Raven doesn't know who she can really trust!

A chance meeting at a bus terminal leads to her delving into the seedy world of strip-clubs, big-ballers and shot-callers.

Now, Raven's shuffling through more men than a Vegas blackjack dealer does a deck of cards. And sex has even become mundane -- little more than a tool to get what she wants.

After a famous acquaintance winds-up dead -- On which shoulder will Raven lean? A wrong choice could cost her life!

There's a reason they call it HOTATLANTA!

"Slick"
DESCRIPTION

Dana & Sylvia have been girlfriends for what seems like forever. They've never been afraid to share everything about their lives and definitely keep each other's secrets ... including hiding Dana's On-The-DL affair from her husband, Jonathan.

Though Sylvia is uncomfortable with her participation in the cover-up and despises the man Dana's creepin' with, she remains a loyal friend. That is, until she finds herself attracted to the very man her friend is deceiving.

As the lines of friendship and matrimonial territory erodes, all hell is about to break loose! Choices have to be made with serious repercussions at stake.

If loving you is wrong, I don't wanna be right!

"SLICK!!! .... Ain't That The Truth! Brenda Hampton's Tale Sizzles With Sensuality, Deception, Greed and So Much Drama – My Gurrll!"

- MYSTERIOUS LUVA, BEST-SELLING AUTHOR OF *SEX A BALLER*

"Dyme Hit List"
DESCRIPTION

Rio Romero Clark, is an Oakland-bred brotha determined to remain a Playa-For Life!

Taught by the best of Macks (his Uncle Lee, Father and Grandfather), Rio feels no woman can resist him. And he knows that his game is definitely tight, considering that he's as a third-generation Playa.

It is Rio's United-Nations-like appreciation for all types and races of women, from the Ghetto-Fab to the Professional, that leads him to the biggest challenge of his Mack-hood, Carmen Massey.

Carmen, a luscious southern-Dyme, at first sight, appears to be just another target on Rio's **Dyme Hit List!** Possessing a body that's bangin' enough to make most brothas beg, mixed with southern-charm that can cause even the best playa to hesitate, Carmen's got Rio in jeopardy of getting his Playa-Card revoked.

Burdened with the weight of potentially not living-up to the family Mack-legacy, Rio must choose between continuing to love his lifestyle or loving Carmen.

Unexpectedly tragedy strikes in Rio's life and a dark secret in Carmen's past ignites a fire that threatens to burn-up their relationship, permanently.

"*Dyme Hit List* is On-Fire with Sensuality! This story is pleasingly-filled with lotsa lip-folding scenes! Curtis Alcutt is a bright new star in fiction!"

-- Winston Chapman, Best-Selling Author of *"Wild Thangz"* and *"Caught Up!"*

"BUSTED" DESCRIPTION

Arianna, Nicole and Janelle each have met a charming man online at LoveMeBlack.com, a popular internet dating website.

Arianna Singleton, a sassy reporter who moves to Philly to further her career as a journalist, finds herself lonely in the big 'City of Brotherly Love' as she seeks a brotha-to-love online. After several comical dates with duds, she thinks she's finally met a stud.

Nicole Harris, a sanctified Public Relations Executive residing in Maryland puts her salvation on-hold when she begins living with a man that she's met on-line. Stumbling across her new beau's e-mails, she realizes that his Internet pursuits didn't end just because they now share the same zip code.

Janelle Carter, a Virginia Hair Salon Owner spends her nights cruising the Web taking on personas of her sexy, confident clients. A business arrangement that she makes on-line brings her face-to-face with a man she thinks is her destiny.

The lives of Arianna, Nicole and Janelle collide in a drama, as they discover that they've all been dating the same man....Chauncey, a brother that makes a habit out of loving and leaving women that he's met thru LoveMeBlack.com.

.
The three of them plot to exact their revenge on the unsuspecting Chauncey, as an unforgettable way of letting him know that he's been ***BUSTED***!

"Rhonda Swan 'brings it' in this comical story that's a warning to wanna-be players as to what can happen if they ever get ***Busted***!"

-- Winston Chapman, Best-Selling Author of *"Wild Thangz"* and *"Caught Up!"*

BLACK PEARL BOOKS INC.

ORDER FORM

Black Pearl Books Inc.
3653-F Flakes Mill Road- PMB 306
Atlanta, Georgia 30034
www. BlackPearlBooks. com

YES, We Ship Directly To Prisons & Correctional Facilities
INSTITUTIONAL CHECKS & MONEY ORDERS ONLY!

TITLE	Price	Quantity	TOTAL
"Caught Up!" by Winston Chapman	$ 14. 95		
"Sex A Baller" by Mysterious Luva	$ 12. 95		
"Wild Thangz" by Winston Chapman	$ 14. 95		
"Crunk" by Bad Boyz	$ 14. 95		
"Hustlin Backwards" by Mike Sanders	$ 14. 95		
"Still Crazy" by Darrin Lowery	$ 14. 95		
"Twisted" by Holland Jones	$ 14. 95		
Sub-Total		$	
SHIPPING: ___ # books x $ 3. 50 ea. (Via US Priority Mail)		$	
GRAND TOTAL		$	

SHIP TO:

Name: _____

Address: _____

Apt or Box #: _____

City: _____ State: _____ Zip: _____

Phone: _____ E-mail: _____